I0555571

A Christmas Reunion

Cauldron Falls

Solara Gordon

Published by THE EARTH MOVED, LLC, 2023.

A CHRISTMAS REUNION

First edition. June 15, 2023.

Copyright © 2023 Solara Gordon.

ISBN: 979-8986032573

Written by Solara Gordon.

Also by Solara Gordon

Cascade Bay
Love Reborn
Reunited By Choice
Love's Triple Play

Cauldron Falls
Believe In Love
A Christmas Reunion

Peyton Corners
Falling for You
Caught by Love's Slow Burn

Standalone
A Heart's Desire
To Love You Again
To Love You Again

Watch for more at https://solaragordon.com/.

DEDICATION:

Thank you to my reader's group and street team, Solara's Glamourous Stars. Your encouragement and suggestions brought Kate and Ryan's story to life. The following receive a special thank you and character named after them: Malia Michel, DeeAnn Kraft, Rebecca Moninghoff, and Chevy (Siobhan) Allen. Your input enriched and added to the story. Thank you all! Solara Gordon

ONE

Ryan Butler looked out across the dance floor. The few couples slow dancing toward the center of the space blocked his view. Kate Ferndale couldn't avoid him much longer. The last two dances of the night were men's choice. All unmatched women were eligible dance partners. Ryan smiled as he caught sight of Kate. The number one rule of the last two dances was no one could turn down the person who asked them to dance.

Kate glanced over her shoulder. Why had she agreed to help with the Christmas Sadie Hawkins dance? Holiday full moon two nights running meant twice the work, twice the number of hopeful couples looking for matches and the loophole rule. All unmatched eligible men and women were potential dance partners, men's choice instead of women's choice. Cauldron Falls' matchmaking council evened the ante every leap year or every two-night full moon. Agnes had assured her months ago that this Christmas wasn't a blue moon one. Two full moons plus two nights each. . .Double Reverse Sadie Hawkins. One night women asked men to dance and looked for matches. Second night, men sought dance partners and looked for matches. The council's decree about men getting the last two dances to make their choices doubled up on everyone.

A few quads and triads amongst the groups mingled at the edge of the dance floor. That evened the count out some. Agnes and her long-time boyfriend Patrick had declared their intent the prior weekend. Six potential couples remained. Seven including her and Ryan. Ryan, her teenage crush, her high school homecoming date,

1

and. . .her reason for moving to Wichita Falls. Ryan saw her as his best friend's cousin. The fourth in their double dates, Franklin and Alicia, her and Ryan. After she overheard his reason for dating her, Kate knew he'd never see her for herself. The young woman who wanted him, found him attractive, was interested in knowing him one on one and date just the two of them. Agnes kept hinting Ryan had changed. Seven years later, so had she. Ryan Butler wasn't getting another chance to break her heart.

Don't be so sure. Here he comes. Great, her conscience couldn't leave well enough alone. Kate turned, picking up her pace, she neared the coat rack. She reached for her coat.

"I would like this dance with you."

She didn't need to turn. She knew who the voice belonged to. Ryan Butler didn't ask. He stated his desire. She could ignore him. Glance at him and say no. Or face him and go. . ."Oh, is that you Ryan Butler?"

Ryan flashed his best smile and offered Kate his hand. "Sure is. Love to dance with you."

Kate gave him a quick once over, glanced down like she was considering his offer. He knew aloof, understood hesitation and didn't mind waiting. He'd get his chance. The chance to hold her in his arms. The chance to declare his intent to the one woman he'd dreamt about, fantasized about and lost his heart to from the moment she'd stolen their first kiss after he'd walked her to her parent's front door post homecoming. They weren't teenagers under someone's watchful patrol. Tonight, under the mistletoe, he'd declare his match choice. Would Kate say yes?

Ryan closed the space between them. "Kate, neither of us is matched or here with a mate. It's male's choice dance. Wouldn't you rather your partner is someone you know?"

Kate looked up. Her hazel eyes caught his attention from the moment his best friend's sister introduced them. Cat eyes are what came to mind. He swore they flashed golden yellow every time she gazed at him thinking he hadn't seen the desire. Her pheromones reached out, swamping him in their passionate embrace, calling out to his wolfish male hormones. Fertility at its highest, oozing off each until the mixture swarmed over them, luring them deeper into its hold. He hadn't said anything then. Not acted on his attraction. Tonight was different. It was the beginning. The beginning of his declared intent and courtship. He'd rather Kate said yes without him needing to spill his gut here in front of the several people watching and overhearing them.

Kate shoved her sweaty palms in her jeans pockets. The other women present were dressed to the nines. Their clothing and mannerisms blatantly screamed mate hunting. Many of them were younger, prettier and—no, she was not putting others above her. She was attractive, pleasant and like Ryan said, unmatched.

The other single unmatched males—well, they were okay. Not too short. Not too tall. A few were older. Some younger. She turned back toward Ryan. There was something to be said about the male that set off a fierce explosion deep in her. Her second sight read Ryan's aura perfectly. Red bursts exploded in firework arrays, tipped with yellows and blues. Reading his aura told her more than if she'd asked him outright what was he thinking. Lust, desire, passion and the thump of pink pulsating close to the middle of his chest. His heart chanted its silent mantra. *I want. I desire. You're the one.*

Kate slowly slid both hands out of her pockets, flexed them and turned toward Ryan until they were toe to toe, barely any space between them. She raised her hand, palm down, hovering it over Ryan's outstretched hand. "This dance is ours."

She laid her palm flat and tight against Ryan's. Clasping his hand tightly, Kate turned. "Follow me. The music is about to envelop us."

Ryan looked at their joined hands. Scalding heat raced up his arm, across his shoulders and shivered down his back. He looked up. A red haze encircled his field of vision. Rhythmic drum beats echoed through him and deep into his psyche. Had Kate bewitched him? Cast a spell over him? Whispers permeated his ears and fled. Words he caught bits and pieces of. It was the males' dance choice. They were supposed to lead. Kate faced him. Her eyes glowed golden, then green, then back to blue. Others could claim their docile women. Confident, strong self-esteem and could hold her own. That was Kate. Not afraid to take a chance when it made sense. Not afraid to take a leap of faith because she believed in herself and for her impossible meant *I am possible*.

Music washed over them as they swayed and turned their way around and across the dance floor. Songs of love, songs of loss, and slow melodious chords played as they reached the darker corner of the dance area close to where he'd first seen Kate.

Kate pulled away. "Are you sure?"

"Oh, yeah. You're the one." Ryan dragged his tongue lightly across each of her knuckles. "Let's find the matchmaker. I'm sure."

"Well, I'm not. Prove me wrong." Kate dropped Ryan's other hand and walked away just like he'd done before. This time her heart wasn't tied up in the outcome or was it?

Kate slipped into the women's restroom. She rushed into the first empty stall, closing the door. Ryan wasn't likely to follow her in here. He might send Agnes in to try to talk her out. Kate leaned against the closed door. Being in Ryan's arms ignited memories, images and feelings. It was like they never parted. Seven years never happened. She clenched her hands at her next thought. She shook her head, flexed her hands, and opened the stall door. No one else was in the restroom. Making her get away might be now or. . . It was now and the back exit off the coat room.

Kate zipped her jacket and fastened her fanny pack around her waist. She leaned out of the coat room entrance. Ryan wasn't anywhere in sight.

Agnes stood close to the coat room entrance. Ryan would question her, drill her for answers. Kate let go a deep sigh. Agnes needed an out. Kate shoved her hand into her jacket pocket, rummaging for a slip of paper. The item she pulled out was a faded business card from her hairdresser. Using the pen on the coat room counter, she scribbled a message on the back of the card. She moved up beside Agnes.

"Don't turn around. I'm leaving. I'm not discussing it. If Ryan drills you for answers, give him this." Kate pushed the business card into Agnes' hand. "I'll call you in a couple days. Good night."

Kate backed up until the shadows of the back hall covered her. As she reached the exit, she glanced back. She didn't need a close-up to know Ryan wasn't happy with what Agnes was saying.

Kate pressed a finger against her lips as she entered the kitchen. Chef nodded, motioning with his hand close to his lips like he was closing a zipper. Pierre held out a take-out bag, nodding as she got closer to the loading dock exit. Pierre leaned close to her, whispering. "Enough for two meals. I stashed a few extra of my chocolate chunk macadamia nut cookies plus a couple pieces of Chef's pumpkin pie with his special amaretto hot chocolate mix in the tin marked important. Enjoy Kate. Merry Christmas!"

"Thanks. Let Aunt Stella know I'll let her know about Christmas dinner in a few days." Kate grabbed the bag and hastily made her way out the exit.

Pierre watched until Kate drove out of the parking lot. He caught Chef watching him as he latched the door.

Chef shook his head. "You know your aunt is going to quiz Kate on her date. Insist she either show up with one or get paired up with some single male relative attending dinner."

"Yeah. To quote Aunt Stella, there's a match for everyone. No matchmaker ever completely retires. Is your cousin Ryan coming?" Pierre latched the exit door and faced Chef.

"He hasn't said yet. I suspect he will. Neither side of our family hardly ever turns down a chance to enjoy Aunt Stella's cooking." Chef slipped his arm around Pierre's waist, briefly hugged him and let go. "Last call time for those that want food to go."

Pierre headed toward the dining area. Kate escaped tonight. Would her getaway last?

TWO

Ryan glanced down at the faded business card laying on his kitchen table. Nothing had changed since Agnes handed him the card. The address was blurred. The salon's name worn off. A cryptic note on the back said he held a clue. He tried calling the number twice. He got a generic voicemail message. He'd left his cell phone number and name asking for the owner to call him. "Damn it, Kate. Why the hide-and-go-seek tactic?"

He pushed his plate away from him. Reheat his coffee and breakfast again? Or barely warm coffee and cold toast, eggs and bacon? Two days of rewarmed food was getting old. He could remake his breakfast or. . .he picked up his plate, put it in the microwave and dumped the cold coffee down the drain.

His mug refilled with hot fresh coffee, his rewarmed breakfast next to him; Ryan opened the notebook in front of him. Business hadn't slowed down since before Thanksgiving. Cauldron Falls' citizens loved their food and parties. Supernaturals celebrated more unofficial holidays and gatherings than the mortal calendar knew of. Pack and Clan formation dates, weddings, anniversaries, major truces and peace treaties, birthdays, and matches filled practically every calendar slot. Some months overflowed with business outsourced to Sadie's and mortal catering businesses. The Cove's bank account was in the black. The last time he entered red figures, he'd vowed to sell the business if things didn't turn around. Praise Lupa for listening.

Ryan jotted several notes next to the date double circled in red and green, December twenty-fifth. Two days after solstice and yule.

7

The blending of mortal and supernatural holidays culminated in a two-weeklong celebration. Past rituals forbade mingling. Much less interspecies contact. Some said deities gasped and laughed with chaotic delight as the first interspecies marriages and families formed. Interbred children thrived and multiplied. Even mortal and supernatural mixes populated Cauldron Falls and the surrounding towns. As the suspicion and disbelief dissipated and acceptance replaced fear and hatred—Ryan smiled. His grandparents, a third-generation mortal witch mix and a mixed-breed shapeshifter, never let their children, grandchildren and great-grandchildren doubt for one moment they were loved, accepted and cherished.

"Aunt Stella, I wish you knew how many I need to cook for. My head chef is off. His assistant is out of town, and I told Pierre I could handle the preparation and cooking on my own." Ryan tossed the pen on the table. He pulled his plate to him and began eating. No missed or cold meals happening today.

Ryan laid his fork and knife on his empty plate fifteen minutes later. He picked up his mug, ready for a coffee refill. Kate filled dreams, late-night dinner menu planning reviews, and the occasional inanity dreams about the meaning of life—Somewhere in the midst of those, a gnome appeared telling him that his future awaited him—left him more tired than if he'd done all of this wide awake after *one* cup of coffee, *not three*.

As he stood, his cell phone vibrated against the table. Dancing in a small arc until the buzzing stopped. Ryan shook his head; whoever it was could call back or leave a voicemail. The shop opened in an hour at ten. The dining room lunch service started at eleven-thirty. Mitchell's email and text left no doubt The Cove would open on time, with hot food ready to serve and plenty of staff helping out. Ryan filled his mug and turned the coffee brewer off.

Buzz! Buzz! His cell phone jangled and vibrated its way across the table, getting closer and closer to the edge. The clink of his coffee mug nudging the edge of his plate sounded as he reached for the cell phone with one hand, trying to stop its fall and setting his mug on the table.

"Shit! That's hot!" Ryan let go of the mug. Wiping his coffee-wet hand on his jeans, he grabbed his cell phone off the table. Who'd texted? Had Barbara and her sister Stephanie called out? They'd asked for the day shift this week, with family arriving on late afternoon flights.

He looked at the text message id. It was the number from the business card. The cryptic message read: You started your detective work, I see.

Ryan scrolled through his most recent messages. Nothing more from that number. He glanced at the screen again, noting the voicemail icon. He quickly dialed his voicemail. Part of him hoped it wasn't Mitchell calling or Nate, the lunch cook. Another part, deep inside, whispered as his voicemail box answered. Maybe it was her. Kate reaching out to tag him, adding he was it again.

"Good start. Keep up the detectiving. Oh, that means looking. I'm impressed *some*."

He knew that voice. Kate wanted a hide-and-seek game. Pluck his nerve and see if he'd play along? He ought to . . .his cell phone rang again. Caller id showed name and number unavailable. He counted to five—pushed the answer button, and put the phone to his ear.

"How can I help you?" he asked in the most sarcastic tone he could muster.

"Ryan Warren Butler, is that any way to speak to me?"

Ryan sat up straighter, silently mouthing, '*Oh shit!*'

"Sorry, Aunt Stella. I thought it was someone else. Prank caller. Your name and number didn't show."

"I'm using Malia's phone. Mine is charging." Stella Stone's voice never failed to reach deep into his core. A retired elementary school teacher and principal never lost her maternal edge. She told him this more than once. His grandmother reminded him Stella got her father's commanding tone and don't give me crap stare down pat. His great great grandfather's military training more than paid off as the next generations came along.

"Now, Ryan," Stella continued. "Why is the Christmas dinner menu not posted on our family website yet?"

Ryan pressed his teeth against his bottom lip. His aunt had taken an age step. Her usually sharp mind and memory weren't what they used to be. She'd forgotten things more frequently like he'd emailed her secretary, Debbie, twice with the menu. Had Debbie lost the menu? He couldn't post it until Aunt Stella approved it. He flipped a few notebook pages back.

"Aunt Stella, I must have missed your or Debbie's email about which menu you approved. I've got the two in front of me. Let's discuss them." Ryan paused, hoping his aunt didn't decide to start fussing at Malia or Debbie.

Aunt Stella cleared her throat. "Ryan, Let's do that. I'll put you on speaker so Malia and Debbie can make notes."

Ryan exhaled deeply, rolled his eyes heavenward and offered a quick thanks to Lupa; his aunt was cooperating. "Sure. Let me know when you're ready."

"Ryan," Malia hastily began. "Please stay away from blaming anyone. Aunt Stella's been on a terror run since Aunt Agatha announced her elopement."

"No worries, Malia. Put me on speaker, and let's get the menu decided." Ryan made a quick note about sending his Aunt Agatha a congratulatory nuptial card and a present. If Agatha had Stella fuming, the person Agatha was marrying must be a doozie.

"Ryan, we're on speaker. Go ahead," Malia said.

Twenty minutes passed as Ryan explained each course and listened to his aunt's feedback. Soup and salad first course items were quick choices, mixed green salad with add-ons of dried cranberries, grated cheddar and goat cheeses, black and green olives plus capers and mushrooms with an ox tail bone broth noodle soup with mixed vegetables. Dressings of raspberry vinaigrette or Caesar ranch. Main course sides were roasted baby red potatoes, three cheese mac and cheese, roasted asparagus, brussels sprouts, and baked sweet potato souffle with cinnamon and melted butter topping.

"Aunt Stella, what do you mean you can't decide on the meat? I've got an entrée for the vegans and vegetarians attending. Pasta shells stuffed with tofu and mushrooms with a tomato basil sauce. None of the bird shifters are attending, you said. Nor are any I'm aware of don't eat pork."

"Why not both?" Debbie offered. "Let the guests choose. I like both."

"You'd eat anything that wouldn't eat you," Stella sarcastically called out.

Ryan gripped his pen tighter. Poor Debbie. His aunt could be a handful when she got in one of her moods. "Aunt Stella, why not both? Makes things easier for you, Debbie and Malia. You don't have to deal with asking and waiting for email responses. I'm doing the cooking and most of the prep."

"Pierre and Chef said they were doing dessert and the bread baskets."

Ryan pressed his lips tighter together. Aunt Stella must be pretty pissed off at her sister Agatha. He wet his lips and acknowledged his aunt's reply.

"Yes, Pierre and Chef are baking the pies, cakes, and bread baskets. Pierre mentioned he was making a double batch of his rum and plum-laced cinnamon rolls for you." He hoped Pierre had the recipe handy and could make two dozen.

"All right. Remember, this is a couples' event. Have you found a date yet?"

Ryan laid his pen down. If he gripped it any tighter, another crack would sound. The pen breaking and the bolt of lightning Lupa was readying to smote him with for creative lying. "Working on it, Aunt Stella."

"Good. I can pair you up with one of the solo females attending. Not all of them are your relatives."

"Thanks, Aunt Stella. I can handle it. I'll post the menu on the family website later today or tomorrow. I gotta answer another call. Bye." Ryan ended the call. His aunt's secondary profession never stopped either. Once a matchmaker, always a matchmaker. Lupa on high, didn't they ever retire? He had to end up with the independent Ph.D. educational instructor, part-time college professor and continuous matchmaker. Non-council approved to hear the family members talk about it. Ryan laid his phone down. A week until Christmas, less than that until Yule and Solstice. Would Malia or Debbie have the guest list to him soon?

BUZZ! BUZZ! His phone started dancing across the table in short bursts. He grabbed the phone, ready to cuss out loud if it was his aunt again. The message indicator blinked. He loosened his grip on the phone as he read Malia's message. *Will get dinner guest total to you in a couple of days. Aunt Stella gave approval to turkey and ham. She wants fish.*

Ryan laid his phone on the table, rose, picked up his dishes and put them in the sink. Cussing, shredding paper, or punching something might release part of his frustrations. Between his aunt and Kate, he wasn't sure who scored highest in plucking his nerve the best. A hot shower and stop by the restaurant might distract him some. Keyword *some*.

THREE

Kate looked up as the bell hanging on the front door of the shop door jingled. She didn't mind covering the front desk while De'Andre's receptionist went to lunch. Rebecca seldom took lunch. The height of the supernatural holiday season spanned the two weeks leading up to Solstice celebrations and the town's park's recreational department Yule log burning festivities. De'Andre and her cousin Josef, the shapeshifter preferred barber, ran the shop from seven A.M. to a couple of hours after dusk six days a week for the two-week stint. Today, five days before Christmas, De'Andre had run out to pick up the lunch she and Josef ordered from their favorite restaurant, The Cove.

"Not hiding very well, are you?"

Kate swallowed hard. What was Ryan doing here? His name wasn't on the appointment list. De'Andre said walk-ins weren't available. Didn't mean Ryan wouldn't try that route. He so loved to do as he desired.

"Not at the moment," she spat out. Glad her hands were beneath the counter. Clenched tighter than her jaw, and sweat slicked. Damn, why did the man ooze pheromones and an aura that sent her inner psyche and feminine core pulsating in response? It wasn't like she hadn't given her sex toys a good workout in the last few days.

"Well, good," Ryan said, smiling as he approached the counter. "Is Josef around?"

"Might be. Why?" Kate sat up straighter, her shoulders back. Crap, she just thrust her breasts at Ryan. Talk about outright mating signal. Could she keep her nipples from pebbling up? She took two

13

breaths and—ah double merde, her psyche and hormones weren't listening one damn iota. Slouching would signal her submissiveness, and that sure the hell wasn't happening. Submissive was not part of her operational design. If Ryan stared at her chest, she'd. . .Ryan's next statement caught her by surprise.

"My cousin Emily and her two tween sons are visiting for the holidays. Josef is the only barber that gets Aaron and Daniel. They are comfortable around him and will let him cut their hair. I'm paying for the cuts and transporting Josef to Emily's sister's place to do the cuts."

Kate pressed her lips together. The Ryan she knew wouldn't have—*Honey, the Ryan you barely know is seven years ago ain't the Ryan standing in front you now. Give 'em a chance.* Great, her psyche, her libido, and her heart kept screaming give him another chance. Why should she? *Darling, 'cuz he's the one. Will you stop fighting the attraction and get on with pursuing?*

She wet her lips, unclenched her hands and nodded. "He's on break waiting for De'Andre to bring back their lunch. She's at picking it up."

"Yeah, I know. She's picking up from my restaurant. She told me Josef was in today." Ryan leaned on the counter. "I can go back and talk with Josef unless you are guarding the entrance."

"I'm what?" Kate raised her hand.

"Assertively guarding the entrance like any dominant would do." Ryan offered his hand palm up.

Great, he wanted peace or was that a piece of. . .her mind wasn't going there. *Oh, but darlin', your mons, clitoris and nipples already have. Why not all of you? Think of the fun you'll have instead of needing new batteries.*

"Traitors," she muttered, slowly lowering her hand. Ryan moved his in sync with hers.

"Who you muttering to? Me or. . ." Ryan slid his palm tightly and hotly across hers, lingering on every move.

Her vision blurred. Bright crimsons, violets and bursts of yellowish orange shot across her field of sight and faded as fast they appeared. She shuddered as heat scampered up her wrist, marking a path upward until it reached her elbow. The warmth stopped pooling as if it waited for her to move, to acknowledge its presence much less direct it anywhere else but back the way it came. Desire, heady and ready to swarm her, failed to heed her retreat command. Upwards it went, not inching nor slowly enveloping each part of her. It raced up her arm, flooding out over her breasts and nipples and overflowed deep into her lower regions. How much moister could her mons and clitoris get? If she moved, would she set off a mini orgasm or a ripple affect that would have her shivering even more?

"Talking to myself. Great habit when I need on-the-spot advice. Problem is losing arguments with myself creates issues cuz you can't unfriend yourself." Kate hurriedly slid her palm off Ryan's, bursts of yellow, pinks and dulled reds outlined her movements.

Ryan snorted. "Let me know how that goes. Been down that road a few times myself. I can use input from others on how not to loose so many of those dang arguments."

Kate pulled her hand away and swiped it on her jeans. "How about you wait here while I let Josef know you're here?"

"No need for that." Josef entered the front of the shop, holding his hand out to Ryan. "I thought I heard Ryan's voice. Come on back."

"I've got a moment before I need to get back to the restaurant." Ryan clasped Josef's hand and moved in for a quick hug. "Emily's in town. Aaron and Daniel need haircuts."

"Come by about three-thirty. My last appointment is at two. Kate, can you please show me out of the shop from three-thirty on?" Josef cuffed Ryan on the shoulder. "Let Emily know the cuts are my solstice gift to her. I've got surprises for Aaron and Daniel too."

"Thanks Josef. I'm prepared to pay for the cuts." Ryan started back toward the shop entrance.

"No need. Emily's a doer and giver. She does a lot for the community and doesn't ask in return. Gifting the cuts is my way of giving back to her as part of the community." Josef held open the door as De'Andre approached.

Ryan nodded as he took one of De'Andre's bags and set it on the counter. "Thanks again, Josef. I'll be back around three-thirty. See you and Kate then."

"See me then? I doubt it." Kate reached for her bag.

"You never know. I might intrigue you enough to wait around for a second impression. May be even a third." Ryan waved to Josef and walked out.

Kate set her bag on the counter. "Josef, I don't know how you do it." Josef reached for his lunch, a BLT on toasted rye bread and a large container of Ryan's made-from-scratch split pea and ham soup. "Do what?"

"Ryan and your friendship." Kate set her diet soda, barbecue-flavored chips, and her three-meat sandwich, freshly made with baked wheat bread on the counter. She handed De'Andre her grilled chicken cobb salad and container of soup.

"First, I like to eat. Ryan is a damn fine chef. Second, our friendship goes way back." Josef pulled one of the lobby chairs over to the counter.

De'Andre set her lunch on the counter and walked over to the door. Flipped the open sign to out to lunch and pulled up a chair to the counter across from Josef. "Ryan isn't so bad. He's good at what he does and knows it. You gotta get to know him. Not the him you remember or think you know."

Kate clapped her hand over her mouth, set her soda on the counter, and gawked at De'Andre. Kate shook her head, pointed at

De'Andre and swallowed her mouth full of soda. "You're damn lucky I didn't spit soda all over us."

Josef chuckled. "I don't know if thank you is needed. I do know that you're blushing, Kate. Nice tinge to your cheeks. You and Ryan gave each other a couple of quick hot once-over looks."

"I did not." Kate popped two chips into her mouth and chewed. How did Josef catch her? Ryan gave her a hot once overlook, twice? She plucked the hem of her top, fanning it some. Deities on high, why couldn't she admit Ryan was gorgeous eye candy? Well worth a few hot once-over looks.

De'Andre laid her fork down. "I caught the way you looked at him as he went out the door. His jeans-encased ass is worth ogling quite a few times. There's something to be said for a man with junk in his trunk, and that ain't the junk in his car trunk."

Kate shook her head. "Okay, so maybe I did enjoy the scenery. So what?"

"Ah, so he scored his second impression," Josef said, opening his soup container. "Let's see if he gets his third. Oh, I got an idea if he gets his third before he gets here later, you gotta tell him."

"No, I don't!" Kate bit into her sandwich. Thinly sliced turkey, ham and pork tenderloin with cranberry and cream cheese spread with cilantro and a dash of southwest seasoning slid across her tastebuds with each chew. A bit of spicy mixed with tang and cooling lingered as she swallowed. Pierre and Chef told her time after time that cooking was almost as passionate as sex. Heady tastes burst forth, igniting reactions that could reach deep into a person's gastronomic soul.

De'Andre pointed her fork full of salad at her. "If you don't, *Josef and I* will."

Kate wiped her mouth, placed both hands on the counter, and leaned forward. "You're gonna what?"

"Tell Ryan you find him sexy, gave him a few hot once-over looks, and want to grab his ass." Josef crumpled his empty soup container and put it in the bag next to him. "I might set you up for a date too." De'Andre chortled. "Matchmaking can be such fun. Think of it as a not-so-blind date."

"De'Andre, I thought you were my friend. Josef, you too." Kate started stuffing her leftovers into the bag they came in.

"Honey, we are. Agnes and we want the best for you. Why not go after what you want?" De'Andre drank the last of her soup and finished her salad.

"Mutual lust, hot desire and lots of chemistry make for a *whoo-hoo* date. If you know what I mean." Josef winked at her as he ate the last of his sandwich.

Kate sat down, wiped her hands on her napkin, and tossed it in the bag holding the trash from Josef and De'Andre's lunch. A date with Ryan, possibly a sexual date? Would that get him out of her system? Convince him that a romantic match wasn't what they were after? She'd have to give it some more thought. Her heart did a pitter-patter dance every time she'd see Ryan. If sex was all she wanted, why had she rushed out of the dance?

FOUR

Emily had tried twice to get Ryan to talk with Josef about not charging for the haircuts. Aaron and Daniel's smiles when she told them Josef was coming to see them lit up the room. They didn't tolerate strangers. Showing them Josef's picture helped each time he came over to cut their hair. Last time Josef had stayed for lunch and played checkers with each of them twice. Today they'd made solstice pictures with Josef after he completed their hair cuts. Each had written a short greeting on their picture. She wished her late wife, Aaron and Daniel's birth mom, could see her boys now. Each was gaining and growing from their home schooling.

"Josef, thank you for coming and cutting the boys' hair. I appreciate your time and energy." Emily held out a tin filled with homemade cookies.

"Emily, you're welcome. You're very welcome. Nancy would be proud. I'm glad she and I were friends. I miss her too." Josef hugged Emily.

Emily knuckled a tear away from her eye as she stepped back. "Some days I swear she is right beside me."

"I understand. If you need anything, please let me know." Josef laid a hand on her arm. "Aaron and Daniel showed an interest in my vacation photos from California. Aaron asked about the weather and mentioned he likes science a lot. Daniel talked about the model car he and his friend put together. I think they're interests are blooming."

Emily nodded. "Yes, soon it's going to be time to decide public school or more home schooling. It's three years since Nancy passed.

19

Aaron and Daniel are talking about spending time with their friends more. I think they're healing and ready to venture out again."

"If I can help, let me know. My nephew and niece attend Cauldron Falls middle school. I'm happy to introduce Aaron and Daniel to them." Josef hugged Emily again, kissed her cheek and stepped back.

Emily cupped his cheek. Tears sparkled her eyes. Her partial smile tugged at his heart. Losing a loved one took time to heal. Losing a spouse even more. He and Emily were close to starting a relationship when Nancy passed. Emily still held a good-sized chunk of his heart. Maybe next Sadie Hawkins full moon, he'd signal his availability and potential match choice.

Ryan pulled into the driveway and honked his horn. Josef had texted him he was ready to go. Ryan smiled as Josef exited Emily's. Aaron, Daniel, and Emily stood on the front porch waving as he and Josef pulled out.

"How'd it go?" Ryan glanced at Josef.

"Okay. Emily didn't break down this time. She mentioned Nancy once. Aaron and Daniel are spending time with friends more. Each gave me a big hug when I finished cutting their hair. Aaron whispered he's interested in a girl down the street. Daniel's new interest is model cars and engines." Josef turned around in the seat, capturing a last glance of Emily and the boys. He let go a long sigh.

Ryan pulled up to the stop sign two blocks away. "Did you ask her? Tell her how you feel?"

"Emily's not ready yet. I'm not sure I'm ready to tell her. Maybe next full moon." Josef turned back in his seat, partially facing Ryan. "Kinda like how you are about telling Kate you're interested."

"*Huh?*" Ryan shot Josef a sideways glance as he entered the highway leading back into town. "I told her. You overheard our banter at the salon."

"Yeah, but you didn't come right out and say hey, I'm interested in you. How about a date?" Josef grinned, adding, "You talked about a second and third impression. Doesn't say much about being interested in more. You know what I mean?"

Ryan picked up speed as they entered the highway and changed lanes. "First, I told Kate at the Sadie Hawkins dance I was ready to see the matchmaker as we danced. Ready to put our names on the matched list. She told me no. Men's dance choice too."

'Dude, that's like getting engaged around here. Declaring your intentions. Kate moved back to town three months ago. She's been dealing with finding work, unpacking and getting reacquainted with Cauldron Falls. Seven years is a long time to be gone." Josef held up his phone. "De'Andre and I think you two need a couple of dates. I managed to snag you a Friday night reservation at Sadie's. You know how hard it is to get that."

"Yes, Siobhan runs a buffet. Pierre and Chef showed me the list for this upcoming Friday. Who do you think got them the recipes and special order items?" Ryan slowed down as he changed lanes.

"Are you bragging or saying you aren't interested in going?"

"If Kate is willing, I am willing. I could ask her myself. I don't need to be set up." Ryan exited the highway and turned on to Main Street.

"Apparently you do. 'Cuz you haven't asked her out. Taking time to say let's get reacquainted. De'Andre is working on getting Kate to say yes to meeting you at Sadie's for a not-so-blind date." Josef put his cell phone back in his jacket pocket.

"Thanks for the vote of confidence. When am I supposed to know if Kate says yes." Ryan pulled into the back alley behind the salon.

"As soon as De'Andre knows, I'll text you." Josef opened the passenger side door. "Thanks for the ride. Appreciate it. I might ask Emily to your aunt's holiday dinner."

"Great, more match making. Aunt Stella will be overjoyed and..." Ryan paused. How did he describe his aunt's zealous nature about matchmaking? Especially after his Aunt Agatha's engagement. Stella wasn't about to let her sister get one up on her. If Aunt Stella would stop ignoring Ethan Hunter's calls and emails, she might be announcing her engagement or elopement. Ethan needed to show up in person and sweep Aunt Stella off her feet again.

"You showing up with a date, and it being Kate will be the topper, I bet. Emily and me. . .well, Aaron and Daniel are going with their dad for Christmas this year. They're kinda excited about it. Seems they got a new baby sibling." Josef got out of the car. "Thanks for the ride. De'Andre will text you with Kate's reply about Friday night."

Ryan gripped the steering wheel tighter with one hand, shot Josef a thumb's up with his other, and curled his lips into the best gee thanks for setting up me grin he could. "Thanks pal. Appreciate the assistance. Talk with you later."

He took his foot off the brake as Josef shut the passenger side door. This afternoon's meeting with Aunt Stella had gone well until she started questioning Debbie and Malia about their dates. There were mumbles about Aunt Agatha and her better not showing up with her fiance looking all kissy-faced about it.

Ryan smirked as he merged into traffic. His short-lived reprieve stopped when he opened the house's front door to leave. Ten minutes later, he promised to inform his aunt of his date's name for printing of the dinner's place cards. Lupa, Kate had to say yes when he got a moment to ask her. He wished she'd stop avoiding him.

"Kate, give me one good reason why you won't go out with Ryan." De'Andre spritzed water on Kate's hair. "You agree he's eye candy worth ogling, worth several hot once-overs, so what's the issue?"

Kate pointed at the mirror. "Looks don't show what's inside. A person's worth, feelings, fears or ethics. I see a reflection of a wet-haired me. No makeup. Baggy sweatshirt, old jeans with holes, and my beat-up gym shoes."

De'Andre sighed and picked up her scissors. "Correct. Why aren't you cutting Ryan the same break?"

Kate lowered her hand. "Because he wanted to rush recording a match. One dance and he's ready to jump the broom. Declare us a couple. That's rushing things."

De'Andre finished trimming Kate's hair. She laid her scissors on the booth's dressing table. "Wow. I didn't know that. But is playing cat and mouse tag any different? You're skittish instead of assertive. Tell him what you want."

"I thought if he had to do some detective work on learning about me, he might. . ." Kate closed her mouth. How was Ryan supposed to get to know her when she hadn't been around for seven years? Who did? Agnes? Her family? Cauldron Falls had changed. It was familiar yet changed in quite a few ways.

"Got you to thinking?" De'Andre started blow-drying Kate's hair.

"Might have taken my fingers out of my ears and listened to what I been saying." Kate drummed her fingers on the chair's armrest. As each fingertip on both hands touched the armrest padding, she counted the current reasons she was avoiding Ryan. Nothing came to mind. She was too caught up in the past to see the present. She and Ryan needed a chance to get reacquainted. De'Andre's and Josef's not-so-blind date made more sense the more she thought about it. "Okay, you're right."

De'Andre turned off the blow dryer. "Right about what?"

"I haven't been fair. Ryan needs a chance to show me who he is. He needs a chance to learn about me. We're not the same person we were seven years ago."

"You're going to go out with him Friday night?" De'Andre laid the blow dryer on the booth's table. She picked up her phone.

"On one condition. We meet each other at the place. There's no need to leave us stuck if we find that things aren't working out." Kate fluffed her hair and stood. "Thanks for the trim. How much do I owe you?"

De'Andre smiled. "Nothing. Consider it part of getting you ready for Friday night. By the way, remember to be prepared. You know if chemistry and passion start percolating."

Kate shook her head as she zipped up her jacket and fastened her fannypack around her waist. "Chemistry might percolate. Nothing says I gotta give in to the temptation."

De'Andre grinned as Kate walked out the door. Forget texting Josef. They had some planning to do.

FIVE

Ryan set his half-empty beer mug on the bar. Siobhan pushed the menu to him. "I'll be back to take your order."

He flipped the menu open. Appetizers, salads, ala carte and entrees lined both pages. The buffet menu covered the menu front. Drinks, alcohol and non-alcoholic, and last call early morning breakfast entrees and to-go items lined the back page.

Two buffet items caught his attention. Meatloaf with Steak Tartar seasoning and roast root vegetables. Chef had augmented the meatloaf recipe he'd learned from a four-star New York restaurant head chef during his culinary school training. Ryan inhaled slowly, letting the kitchen scents fill his nostrils and sashay across his tastebuds. His wolf half howled deep within his psyche. Tonight's new moon reached deep into him, touching his hormones, his animal half and kindling the yearn to mate. To claim his fated mate like his granddad had done with grandmama. Kidnapping was verboten by pack and human law. Grandmama went willingly with Granddad. His story about restraining her and carrying her out of her college dorm over his shoulder was make-believe. She pushed him out on the loading dock strapped to a two-wheel dolly covered with a sheet. Ryan grinned. Eloping was hard when the pack alpha's guards and second in command were watching. Granddad knew what he was giving up when he resigned his leadership.

Ryan glanced toward the front door as it opened. Where was Kate? He waited out front for her like they'd agreed. She wasn't standing him up, was she?

25

Siobhan entered the kitchen and sat on the stool next to Kate. "How long do you expect Ryan to wait?"

Kate sighed. "I don't. I said I'd meet him. Have dinner and talk. Why I've got the jitters? Don't know."

Chef held out a shot glass filled with an amber liquid. "This will calm your nerves. Aged golden apple cider. A bit of kick, some nectar for your sweet tooth, and a blast of warmth in the belly."

Kate reached for the glass. "How aged? Some of this kicks like a mule. No need to get euphoric."

Siobhan laughed. "Jitters calmed, yes. Tipsy, no. It's less than a month old."

Kate took the glass, saluted Siobhan, Pierre and Chef. She waved her hand over the glass, sniffing the cider's aroma. Sweetness plus the apple's tangy tickled her nostrils. She took a sip. Sugary goodness rolled across her tastebuds and pooled at the back of her throat. She swallowed, blinked and shook her head. Warmth exploded, cascading like a roller coaster down an incline, straight into her stomach. She blinked twice and held the glass out to Siobhan. "I think that was enough."

Siobhan shook her head. "Chef neglected to give you a spoon to stir it up. Liquor pools close to the top if you don't mix it up. Hits you like a shot of brandy. Ignites a fire ball across your tongue, down your throat and landing in the pit of your belly."

Kate puckered her lips and blew air out. "I need ice water."

Pierre took the glass. "No."

"No?" Kate whispered, in a very hoarse voice.

"No," Siobhan repeated, standing up.

Chef stepped around them, holding another shot glass. Kate arched an eyebrow, scowled at Chef and pointed at the glass. "No more," she managed to croak out.

"It's milk. Ice-cold milk. It'll cool your tongue and tastebuds plus calm your throat and stomach." Chef held the glass out to her.

Kate clasped the glass with two hands, eyeing the contents. No odors. White-colored liquid greeted her as she held the glass up. "Milk?" She glanced at Siobhan, Pierre and Chef. All three nodded. Kate inhaled, slowly exhaled and gulped.

Coldness swamped her tongue, putting out multiple smoldering patches of blazing heat until is slid down her throat and into her stomach. She closed her eyes, drank more until the glass was empty. She slowly opened her eyes, jerked and quickly set the glass on the counter close to her. Shivers roared up and outward, swamping her in their ripples as she chafed her arms. She continued chafing for several more moments. "Damn, I ain't getting near aged golden apple cider again."

Pierre chuckled. "You forgot about your jitters. 'Sides, once you eat, you'll be fine. The cider is less than two proof."

Kate glared at Pierre. "Good thing we're cousins. Otherwise I'd. . ." She stopped talking. She shook her head, grinned and spoke again. "That cure is one I don't care to repeat."

Chef nodded. "None of us do. Sometimes the best medicine is the kind that distracts you."

Siobhan patted Kate's shoulder. "Come on. I'll get your and Ryan's order. There's a corner table near the bar where the two of you can easily hear each other. Dinner hour can get a bit rambunctious."

Kate stood. Chef was right. She needed to eat, and his meatloaf with steak tartar seasoning was one of her favorite Sadie's meals.

Siobhan held open the kitchen door. "Ryan is sitting at the bar near the front door. Go ahead and sit at the table middle way toward the front. I'll bring him over."

Kate followed Siobhan out of the kitchen. She paused by to the table with the reserved sign. "Have a seat. Ryan will be back in a moment."

Siobhan continued toward the front of the bar. Kate sat down, wiping her hands on her jeans twice. Sweaty palms, stomach butterflies, and . . .

Ryan stood next to the table. Kate flexed her hands and started to stand.

"Going to run away?" Ryan sat in the chair across from her.

"No, ready to introduce myself. Habit." Kate slowly sat back in her chair.

"A starting point." Ryan held out his hand. "Evening, ma'am. I'm Ryan Butler. Nice to meet you."

Kate looked down and back up at him twice. How long was this going to go on?

Kate reached out, took hold of his hand and shook it. "I'm Kate Ferndale. Good to meet you Ryan Butler."

"Okay, you got the introductions out of the way. Time to place your orders." Siobhan slid a menu in front of each of them.

Kate pushed the menu back toward Siobhan. "Meatloaf special with green bean casserole, mashed potatoes and a couple of yeast dinner rolls with cinnamon butter. Water to drink."

Siobhan nodded. "Brown gravy or pan-dripping gravy?"

"Pan dripping." Kate turned to Ryan. "Split a salad appetizer?"

"Sure. What dressing?" Ryan handed Siobhan his menu.

"Orange Honey Cilantro. A bit of sweet mixed with tang and heat. No croutons or onions." Kate smoothed her napkin across her lap.

"Sounds good." Ryan looked at Siobhan. "I'll have the meatloaf special too. Roasted asparagus and mashed potatoes with brown gravy. Water for me too."

"All right. Two meatloaf specials. Two mashed potatoes. One green bean casserole. One roast asparagus. Pan dripping gravy on one mashed and the other brown." Siobhan tucked the two menus under her arm. "I'll bring out the rolls, cinnamon butter and salad plus your waters in a moment."

Ryan waited until Siobhan was out of earshot. "Niceties aside. Why did you come out of the kitchen?"

Kate placed her folded hands on the table. She didn't say anything. Just kept looking at him. He rubbed his lips together, inhaled and exhaled slowly. Maybe a different question? He opened his mouth when Kate replied.

"Jitters." Kate pointed at him. "You're not a blind date. Yet it sorta is."

Ryan nodded. "Yeah. True in a lot of ways. How do we break the ice?"

Kate snickered and leaned back in her chair. "We already have. Might be time to ask the hard questions. You know the ones of where you been, why did you move, and who are we now."

"I didn't move. I've traveled, studied, and wondered why I didn't pursue you after you moved." Ryan picked up his fork. "Siobhan approaches with our salad, rolls and waters."

Siobhan set the salad and rolls middle of the table between their glasses of water. "Chef is making up a new batch of cinnamon butter. I'll be back with it shortly."

Kate glanced over her shoulder. Siobhan was talking with patrons at the bar.

Kate hadn't figured on having others overhear her and Ryan's discussion. She speared a fork full of salad and spoke. "The thought passed through my mind a few times. Truth is I needed to get away. Cauldron Falls didn't have much to offer me then. Get bonded, kids, and maybe open a business or become a matchmaker. Not many options. I wanted to see what was beyond Cauldron Falls."

"Traveling couldn't do that?" Ryan ate some salad. Keeping his mouth full for the next moment or two might keep his crash-ass thought from blasting forth. His and Kate's break up still stung when his teenage ego tried to take over. He needed to hear her out. Let go of the past and focus on the here and now.

"Something I never shared with you was my family class within the Witches Coven. Second class red zone. Few magic traits, natural mages of mortal ancestry. . .You know the differences the older generations used to set themselves apart." Kate ate two more bites of salad and laid her fork down.

"Used to protect them. Set them apart in their minds. Your aura reading and healing crystal magic stood up to the best of them." Ryan finished the rest of the salad, put his fork down, and drank some water. Now if he could keep his mind off Kate's fertility and pheromones tantalizing him, he might not crack the table gripping it any harder.

"At some point, I had to escape. Find me and determine who I was. Don't know if that makes sense." Kate set her half-full glass down.

"It does. I traveled to get away. Sometimes two to three months away, working with my cousin Victor Adams as roadies. Met lots of bands, saw a lot of places, and got to know people who didn't ask about me being an Alpha's nephew or his brother's kid. I got to be me." Ryan split one of the rolls, holding half out to Kate.

Their fingers touched as she took the roll. A burst of red mixed with yellow sparked from her fingers to Ryan's and back. Ryan drew back his hand, glancing from her to his hand and back up. What had just happened?

"Did you see that?" Ryan turned his hand over.

"See what?" Kate tore her roll half in two. "What you looking for?"

"Come one, Kate. You see auras and read them. Use crystal energy color." Ryan placed his hand on the table. "You bsing me you missed those sparks? The yellows and reds?"

"Oh, that. Probably static sparks." Kate popped part of her roll into her mouth.

Ryan pressed his lips together. Aura sparks reading was one of the lesser magic traits in his family. His Aunt Agatha said she knew Derek Fox was her match from the aura love sparks they ignited every time they touched. Lupa, wasn't even a full moon and the sparks were happening.

SIX

Ryan had changed the subject by the time Siobhan returned with their meals and the cinnamon butter. Kate's vague answer about aura sparks being a minor coincidence said more than if she'd admitted she'd seen and felt them. Her startled reaction caught his attention almost as much as the sparks had.

"Kate, why did you come back?" Ryan cut into his slice of meatloaf. Beginning here and now meant asking the hard questions and his willingness to hear Kate's answers. His focus needed to be actively on her. Staring at her as they ate wasn't going to do that.

Kate laid her fork down, wiped her mouth, and picked up her water glass. "Wichita Springs and Chicago tempted me with worldly things. Large city, bright lights and possibilities that Cauldron Falls never had. It hit me in the still of the night after the umpteenth hollow no connection date. I wanted and needed a home with friends and family around me."

Ryan nodded. "I get it. I came back from my last trip to find my family needed me. My uncle, the pack's alpha, had stepped down. Victor, me and Mateo refused the alpha role. Zack, my nephew, is our temporary Alpha. There's a movement to name co-alphas. A man and woman to lead."

"We came back to find what we thought from our past was what we needed now. The person I was then isn't who I am now." Kate finished her meatloaf and potatoes.

Ryan laid his utensils on his empty plate. "What do you think about us starting over?"

32

Kate picked up one of the remaining rolls, tore it in two and held up both pieces. "What this roll was isn't anymore. Each half is now unique and changed. You can put them side by side without the tear showing. That doesn't make them what they were. Do you get why I challenged you to do the detective work?"

Ryan gripped his napkin. Whatever he said could make or break things. Kate watched him intently. He had to say something. Or the evening was shot.

He swallowed the last of his water, leaned back in his chair and replied. "You want me to get to know you. See you for who you are now, not the Kate from our past. Not my memories. Makes what De'Andre and Josef said make sense. We have the choice and chance to make a second first impression here and now."

Kate pointed at him. "And do it our way. Forget the old standards. We set our own standards. We agree upon the foundation we start from and go from there."

Ryan slowly exhaled. Holding his breath wouldn't change what his ego and zealous male id kept screaming. Kate turned him on. Even with her aloof chilled manner, chemistry was happening. Fertile pheromones reached out, tickled his nostrils and smacked his male hormones into overdrive. His wolf howled each time he inhaled her scent. How much more could he withstand?

He pressed his fingertips against the table as he spoke. "If I agree to this, there is one cardinal thing I believe is a must."

Kate lowered her hand. "What's that?"

"Sex. No denying attraction. No bsing each other. If we mutually choose to act on our attraction and desire, we're upfront about it." Ryan slowly lifted his hand off the table. He'd silenced his wolf for a moment. His keen inner sense watched Kate's eyes and movements. She'd given him several hot up-and-down glances. Her pheromonal output increased every time she did. "Unless you're not attracted to me. I wouldn't believe you if you said that. You wouldn't be here if you didn't."

Kate worried the inside of her lower lip between her teeth. She'd forgotten how well Ryan could read her. His inner wolf aura flashed red and gold from the moment he saw her at the dance Saturday night. She'd witnessed her own aura sparks as she looked in the mirror trying to calm herself before she'd snuck out. Denying attraction wasn't going to work. They'd known that the first time they'd paired up. Chemistry sparked other things. Ryan was right that stifling their shared desire and attraction wouldn't help their second chance if they decided to make that leap of faith.

"I don't scratch itches for no reason. I learned I'm a lover. Sex is good stuff. I need more." Kate leaned back in her chair. She drained her water glass. She'd almost said the f word. The one word she learned that cheapened sex between two friends who cared deeply for each other. Too many takers had tried to get her to do the dirty and walk away. Six long months the last time she did that. Six months until her heart stopped aching and she knew she needed more than physical release to contemplate sex again.

"Duly noted. I didn't mean here and now. Siobhan would grab us by our neck scruffs and waistbands and toss us in the garbage dumpster with no qualms. She keeps an extra one full of cold water to flash cool things off. Seen her, Pierre and Chef do it a few times." Ryan winked as he added, "Her boyfriend Ty has pitched in from time to time too."

Kate smirked. "Figured you had manners after a few of your Aunt Stella's lectures."

Ryan nodded. "Speaking of her, I see your name is on the annual Christmas dinner list."

"Her genealogy hobby hit pay dirt to quote her. I'm a distant relative twice removed on Agatha's side. I got the call 'cuz Stella wasn't going to let Agatha beat her at matchmaking this year." Kate pulled her phone out of her fanny pack. "How did you see the list?" "I'm doing the cooking. Pierre and Chef are doing breadbaskets and desserts." Ryan sighed. "All that's left is finding a dinner date. And to quote Malia, Stella's gonna know if any of us are faking things."

"Couldn't you go with a friend and that be enough?" Kate laid her phone on the table.

"In the past, yeah. Now that Aunt Agatha announced her engagement and possible elopement, Aunt Stella is out to top the matchmaking numbers from last year and find herself a match too." Ryan glanced at his watch. "Before it gets too late, let's walk over to The Cove and have a piece of my pastry chef's rum cake. It's quieter and we can talk about where we go from here."

Kate reached for the bill Siobhan laid on the table as she passed with another table's order. "I'm game with one hesitation."

Ryan laid money on the table next to the bill. "I'm listening."

"We let Siobhan know. That way our cars are safe in the parking lot. Valet won't have them towed. *And*—I hope Ben made some of his brandied ice cream to go with it." Kate picked up the money and the bill.

Ryan nodded and grinned. "I agree. Ben said he was working on a new flavor to go with the cake. Brandy Rum Ripple I think is what he said."

"Sounds like a new dessert in the making." Kate approached the bar where Siobhan stood talking to her boyfriend Ty.

"Siobhan, put the change in the charity tip jar. I hope you make the two hundred dollar goal. Brandle Fields Sanctuary needs all the help it can get." Kate turned as Ryan reached her side. "How about a charity tip jar at The Cove?"

"Already got one. Pets need help and care. The great part is hooking up teen shapeshifters with a pet. Learning about how to care for them instills respect and a deeper understanding of their duality vs. someone who isn't." Ryan shook Ty's hand.

"Siobhan, we'll be back for our cars. We're going to The Cove for dessert and talk a bit more." Kate fastened her fannypack around her waist.

Siobhan put the change in the charity tip jar. "Thanks for the donation. We're over two hundred and on to our second two hundred. Don't worry about your cars."

"Lance, Keith and I will check on them in a bit. Enjoy your dessert." Ty waved as Kate and Ryan walked toward the exit. "Fertility rolling off those two like a couple of—"

Siobhan clapped her hand over Ty's mouth. "No need to announce it. I'm sure they know. Josef and De'Andre need our help in giving them the time and space to reunite. You know a second chance?"

Ty nodded as he nipped Siobhan's palm. She pulled her hand away. Ty grinned."Like you and me and. . .let's say learning limits, safe words and understanding who's in charge."

Siobhan leaned on the bar, closing the space between her and Ty. "Yeah, spanking your naughty ass does help fire things up."

"You haven't done that." Ty pulled back.

"Try it. You might like it." Siobhan winked, turned and walked into the kitchen.

Ty slid off the bar stool, glanced around, and shoved his hands into his jeans pockets, trying to keep his briefs, cock and zipper from getting any friendlier. He caught one last glimpse of Ryan and Kate as they exited Sadie's. Maybe second chances happened when one least expected it.

Ryan pushed the crosswalk button as he and Kate reached the corner. "It's almost eerie the difference in noise levels. I hear the traffic and other sounds. The moments of quiet are like balloons popping."

Kate snickered. "I get it. Sometimes we get lost in the inner and outer noise going on in life."

Ryan pointed to the crosswalk sign as it changed. "We take things for granted cuz that's the way everyone does them. Like waiting for the crosswalk sign to change."

"Which is why we're going to The Cove to talk. If we had stayed at Sadie's, everyone would be watching. There's Ryan and Kate. Are they getting back together? What's up with them?" Kate stepped off the curb. "Sometimes you gotta get out of the limelight and do your own thing."

Ryan matched his pace to Kate's as they finished crossing the street. He clasped Kate's wrist. "Then you won't mind me doing this."

SEVEN

Ryan moved into the building entrance, pulling Kate closer. He glanced behind him as he tugged her to him. "We're slipping into the shadows. I'm doing my own thing."

Kate's breath wafted across his face as he faced her. He slipped his arm around her waist, leaned closer, pressed his lips to hers, and pulled back. "Nice."

"Did you just kiss me?" Kate didn't move.

"Yes, I did. Practice run." Ryan leaned closer. "Now for the real thing."

Kate blinked. Ryan, lips puckered, came toward her. Few could see them if any stopped to gawk at them in the cornered shadow of the building's entrance. Doing their own thing was right. Making out like a couple of teens letting their hormones drive—what did it matter. They were in charge. Kate tilted her head opposite Ryan's and pressed her lips against his.

Ryan cradled her against him, deepening the kiss. His lips opened. The tip of his tongue roved over her lips, seeking, tasting and asking for more. Kate slipped one arm around Ryan, nestling closer. She looped her other arm around his shoulders, threading her fingers into his hair.

Ryan pressed tighter to Kate. With every breath, they touched more. It was like their clothing disappeared and they stood stark naked deep in their psyches. Kate's lips parted, her tongue met his. Deep within, his wolf growled, panting with desire, wanting to claim his mate. Ryan pulled back. Kate's fertile scent marked him,

38

soaking him inside and out, dousing him deep into his heart. Much more and his wolf would demand control.

"Kate, I think we need to stop." Ryan slowly lowered his arms. He'd come close to grinding against her. Pushing her back against the building and . . .doing a clothes-on mating dance. One that could have them asking for bail money if Cauldron Falls' finest caught them in the act. Not where he wanted to end the evening.

Kate opened her eyes. She inhaled slowly. Male pheromones slid up her nostrils and deep into her psyche. She blinked twice. Ryan hadn't affected her like this since. . .the last time they'd sated their sexual desire, a month before she moved to Witchita Springs. Ryan wouldn't discuss committing or offered any solutions to them continuing what they had. His focus was going on the road and seeing what the world was like outside of Cauldron Falls. Similar to her desire and focus had to be somewhere different and experience life away from home.

"Stop like we did before?" Kate started to step back. Ryan moved with her.

"Thought we were on the here and now?" Ryan kept his hands on her shoulders.

"A little hard to do when our connection ignites." Kate gripped Ryan's arms and backed away from him. She let go of his arms as she continued backing away.

"Connection isn't bad." Ryan took several quick breaths before he spoke again. "Do we control it or it control us?"

Kate wiped her palms on her jeans. "We're in control."

Ryan nodded as he stepped out into the light illuminating the sidewalk. "Agreed. I think we've earned a hot toddy with our cake and ice cream. Ben's usually got a pot of his special decaf going about this time. How about a cup?"

Kate chafed her arms. Between the wind and putting space between her and Ryan, a chill enveloped her. "Hot toddy sounds good. I may forgo the ice cream tonight. Cake and a warm drink sound good."

Ryan moved up beside her, offering his hand. "I do want to get reacquainted. I prefer to attend Christmas dinner with you as my date. Makes things easier when you know the person you're there with."

"Sure is. If I do go with you, we're not agreeing to any match or a full moon bonding." Kate clasped Ryan's hand. Warmth massaged their palms, slowly wrapped itself around their wrists and dissipated.

Ryan raised their joined hands. "I agree. We're going as friends. Family friends. Just know Aunt Stella and Aunt Agatha are going to push hard for why."

"Matchmakers don't like to hear no to their attempts at matchmaking." Kate paused as they reached The Cove's entrance and faced Ryan. "That's another reason why I moved to Witchita Springs. No one prodding me about not being matched."

"Oh?" Ryan opened the door, waiting for her to say more.

"I didn't want then and I don't now want someone matchmaking me. I make my own choices. Some of the family tried to set you and me up; I found out after we split." Kate entered The Cove hoping her last statements caught Ryan by surprise as much as it had her when she heard about it from two of her cousins twice removed.

Ryan shook his head. Matchmaking energy ran hot and heavy with every full moon. Full moon sparks igniting and love magic pulsating—chemistry happened. Attraction peaked, and ripples of desire mixed with intent flooded everyone. Mortal and supernatural felt the lure. Supernaturals more. Magic practitioners tried to resist. No wonder the Matchmakers Council issued the edict creating Sadie Hawkins events. When prospective males' pent-up hormones mixed with female fertility. . .Ryan smiled. The emotional and hormonal flood knew no limits. Everyone was susceptible. Controlling the flood and learning how was key to not making a stupid match. Thirty days matched to someone you only wanted to jump their bones, and nothing else hit hard when the flood dried up.

He followed Kate into The Cove's entryway. He blinked twice as his vision adjusted to the lighting. The chatter of diners reached him as he stepped around Kate and began making his way to the kitchen. Several of the wait staff nodded as they passed him. Ryan paused and glanced behind him. Kate followed tight in his wake. The closer they got to the kitchen, the more noticeable the squeak of the swinging kitchen door got.

The door swung open, banging forcefully against the wall. A robust gray-haired man wiping his hand on his apron exited the kitchen. Mitchell Harrison shielded his eyes, grinned and pointed at Ryan. "About time you showed up."

"Eh, long lunch." Ryan clasped Mitchell's hand. "Full crowd. How'd lunch go?"

"Busy. A few of our regulars. Third Circle Cover bridge game. Matt and Ruben plus two of their grandsons came in for their weekly chess matches." Mitchell leaned on the counter. "How'd the..." He stopped talking as Kate moved up beside Ryan.

"Evening Mitchell." Kate sat on a stool between Ryan and Mitchell. "Is Ben in?"

"Yep. Prepping tomorrow's breakfast menu and planning what sweetbreads he's going to offer." Mitchell looked at the kitchen door. "I told him to take a break. He's been here since six this morning. Told him there's more to life than work."

Ryan chuckled. "Creativity is juicy for us. Our's is baking, meal planning and cooking."

"I thought I smelled bagels when the kitchen door swung open. Are there any left from this morning?" Kate pulled her wallet out of her fanny pack.

Mitchell pushed the kitchen door open. "Let's go ask him. Unless you are planning on staying out here."

"No, we're here for a scoop of Ben's latest ice cream creation, a hot toddy and maybe a piece of his rum cake if there's any left." Ryan held the door after Mitchell entered the kitchen. "Kate, you coming?"

Kate put her wallet back in her fanny pack, stood and nodded. With Mitchell and Ben around, she and Ryan didn't have to worry about more sparks and pheromonal heat happening. She hoped.

Ryan let the kitchen door swing shut behind him after Kate entered. Her sideways glances as she moved past him smoldered in ways only those who knew her would catch on. His wolf vision kicked in as they cuddled and kissed in the shadows. Reds and yellows outlined Kate like an infrared motion detector. Heat rose off her, floating in a pool around her until his burst arced out, mixing with hers. No wonder a cloud of desire and want enveloped them. Residues of the earlier strong bright aura sparks enhanced by their basic chemical pheromonal attraction equaled—lust?

Kate rubbed her finger under her nose. Male hormonal scents swirled around her, flirting with her psyche and demanding responses. She'd caught part of Mitchell's as they stood talking. He smelled of food, spices and starched clothing. The other male help scents whizzed past her as each server entered and exited the kitchen. Their hormones and pheromones briefly touched her, following in their owner's wake. One stood out. There was no mistaking his aftershave, his male lure and bold chemistry reaching out, touching her as it could and attempting to mark her. Ryan's wolf had claimed her. Placed his psyche's scent on her in a way only one type of magic could. Full moon sparks. Blue moon love sparks plus a Sadie Hawkins event, and. . .she'd gotten marked. Magically marked by love sparks and full moon magic. Great, how did she deal with this and keep her wits about her?

Darlin', you put me in charge. Kate snorted. Put her psyche in charge? Right, she'd end up hooked up with Ryan and matched before she could say no way. Chemistry was awesome. Attraction great. When the hormones and pheromones stopped percolating, then what? Some of her friends had rushed into full moon matches, only to regret their decision halfway through the thirty-day commitment period. Could she and Ryan keep their wits about them? Make levelheaded decisions?

"Kate," Ryan nudged her. "My office is over here. Mitchell is letting Ben know we're here." Ryan pointed to an open door close to the hallway leading to the loading dock entrance.

"Sounds good. Lead the way." Kate followed Ryan as he made his way around the serving area.

Ryan shut the office door and faced Kate. "You okay? You seem preoccupied out there."

Kate sat in the chair closest to the desk. "I'm fine. My psyche is kicking. My nose is twitching, and auras are off the chart. Colors are mixing and sparking off people like fireworks going off."

"Another full moon isn't until next weekend." Ryan sat in the chair next to Kate. "Did this happen last weekend?"

Kate shrugged. "I see auras most of the time. I usually don't think much about it. It's like your wolf sense nuzzling you. You know it's there."

"Sixth sense-making itself known. Lot of matches happened my cousin Malia told me. Aunt Stella keeps up on all the matchmaker gossip and reports." Ryan looked up as the office door opened.

Kate smiled and nodded. "Aunt Agatha does the same. She reported something to my grandmother. I tuned it out. Especially when the why wasn't my name on the list portion started."

EIGHT

Ben entered carrying a tray with two mugs on it plus a medium-sized brown paper bag. "Hey Kate, got your bagels here. On the house. Hot decaf tea in the mugs. My private stash. Don't tell Mitchell. Hi boss man."

"Evening Ben." Ryan took the tray from Ben and set it on the desk.

"Mitchell is getting the cake out of the oven. Fresh pieces for both of you in a moment. Ice cream sold out within the first two hours of dinner rush." Ben dropped into the chair behind the desk. "Ryan, I got a question for you."

Ryan perched on the corner of the desk. "No, you can't buy me out. What's your other question?"

Ben laughed. "Breakfast rush is growing. I think we need to look at expanding the menu and me working morning rush. Mitchell is good with baking the bagels and muffins if I've got them prepped. Nate is good with coming in mid-morning and working the lunch rush with me. He doesn't mind working late if needed."

"Single and young. Work fulfills a lot of the empty hours." Ryan shook his head. "I keep telling Nate there's more to life than work and sports."

"I hear he's been dating my daughter's teacher. I don't ask. Melissa keeps asking me when I am going to get matched." Ben stood up. "Geez, when your own daughter starts, you know these Blue Moon and double fulls are pumping out extra sparks."

Ben offered Ryan his hand. "Let me know what you think about making up the switches. Nate is good with making the switch next week if you agree. Meanwhile, I got a menu to finish and get home

44

to Melissa before she gets more matchmaking advice from my mother."

Ryan shook Ben's hand. "I'm good with the switch. I'll talk with Nate in a couple of days. Thanks for taking on the expanded breakfast menu and rush."

"We're all owners here. Looking out for the business is key to its continued success." Ben opened the office door. "Kate, good seeing you. I put some of my new cream cheese mix in there. Strawberries, blueberries and cinnamon mix. Let me know how you like it."

"Thanks, Ben. I will let you know. Good seeing you again."

Ryan left the door ajar after Ben exited. "Hope Mitchell brings the cake soon."

Kate pulled one of the mugs to her. She inhaled and wrapped her hands around the mug. "Mulberry, apple, and a hint of nutmeg. Reminds me of a wine I used to get from a winery in Witchita Springs."

Ryan picked up his mug and sipped. "Sweet with a bit of tart. Nice mixture. Ben is thinking about selling tins of his blends as part of the notions section you saw up front."

Two rapid knocks sounded. Mitchell called out. "Cake inbound. Found a bit of rum bourbon-flavored whip cream for each piece. Enjoy. I got a dishwasher waiting."

Kate tittered at Mitchell's last statement. "Sounds like you got an ornery appliance."

Ryan smiled and nodded as he sat down. "Newly installed. Mitchell is the only one who's read the manual cover to cover. He's slowly teaching others how to run it. Not that it is that difficult."

"New toy aspect. Had a co-worker that thought taking on all the new positions was a fast track to getting a promotion. Last I heard from him, he was with a different company and laying low." Kate cut into her piece of cake. "Here's to more discussion, I suppose."

Ryan held up his fork full of cake. "Yes, more discussion. Here's to a mutually satisfactory outcome."

He waited until Kate's gaze met his after several moments of quiet eating and drinking. Ryan wiped his mouth with his napkin, laid his fork on his empty plate and turned sideways in the chair so he faced Kate head-on.

"Two things I think we know for sure." He held up two fingers. " First, our chemistry and attraction are strong."

Kate nodded. "Agreed. We wouldn't have kissed each other if that wasn't there."

"Good." Ryan lowered one finger. "Second, we're talking. We've sorta agreed we need time to get reacquainted. I have a small addendum to that."

Kate set her empty tea mug down. "What's that?"

"We tell our matchmaking relatives we're going to the dinner together to get them off our backs. We can use the time leading up to the dinner to sorta date." Ryan laid a hand on the desk.

"Sorta date?" Kate pushed her chair back, creating space between them. Ryan's aura changed color four times during his last two statements. Mauve, the passion color, tinged the outer edge of his aura silhouette twice. Knowing where his passion was on what he said might help her calm her jittery stomach.

"With three days before Christmas, do you think we're going to be able to reacquainted enough to say yeah, we're together again?" Ryan stacked their plates, utensils and mugs on the tray Mitchell left on the desk.

Kate nibbled her lips, wet them and slowly swallowed. Two words came to mind practice or fake it until she and Ryan convinced themselves and their immediate friends they were attempting a reunion. "We're going to have to do a lot of practicing. You know, make sure we've got each other's stories down and why we're giving this a go again."

Ryan ran his hands through his hair. "Aunt Stella's bullshit meter will pick up on a bald-faced lie before you say two words."

"Aunt Agatha too. Even my mom and grandmother. Deity on high, the interlace of cousins and matchmakers. Ryan, maybe we can go as friends?" Kate stood up.

"We could, but—" Ryan stopped talking. He shrugged and rose.

"For the family matchmaking matriarchs, that isn't good enough." Kate sighed.

Ryan pushed the office door open. "For dinner, we'd be okay. Beyond that. . . with Aunt Agatha and Aunt Stella trying to see who can get the most matches before the next full moon, we gotta do more than friends."

"Friends with benefits might buy us a reprieve." Kate shook her head as she continued speaking. "Then comes the blasted are you pregnant questions. No one minds their own damn business. This is one key reason I moved. I needed to find me. Not get bartered off because the match seemed advantageous to both families."

Ryan pointed toward the loading dock exit. "We can cut through the back parking lot that connects Sadie's and The Cove parking areas. We can talk more in a moment."

Kate waved to Mitchell and Ben before she followed Ryan out onto the loading dock. Ryan held out his hand. "It's starting to sleet. We're gonna have to make a run for it. I say let's meet up at one of our places and discuss this more tomorrow evening. Our second unofficial date."

"Spending time together is part of this. Sure, I can cook dinner. You bring dessert?" Kate carefully made her way down the loading dock steps, holding onto Ryan's hand.

"Ben should have more ice cream made by then. I'm good with bringing dessert." Ryan pulled her to him, adding in a whisper hotly against her ear. "I'll bring protection too. We won't have to worry about holding back if our chemistry erupts."

Kate put her hands on Ryan's shoulders and pushed. "Don't let your gonads overheat. Nothing says the catalysts will keep igniting once we get naked."

"Careful. It's getting slicker." Ryan tightened his hold on her waist. "We've seen each other naked. Nothing cooled then. I doubt it will now."

Kate laughed, slowly moving around Ryan. "We're older. Bodies change. If we get to the naked part, leave room for surprises."

Ryan shrugged. "Okay. We gotta focus on getting to our cars."

Kate slid one foot across the wet pavement in front of her. Her foot kept going. "Crap. The ice is sticking. How are we going to get to our cars this way?"

"Stay put. I'll get some ice melt and sprinkle it as we go." Ryan made his way partway back up the loading dock steps. He came back down carrying a small container. "Not much ice melt in here. I'll get my car, come get you and take you to your car. Go on back up the steps. There's a chair close to the door you can sit on until I get back."

Kate took the steps one at a time, testing each for slickness. Back on the loading dock, she turned around. "Ryan, don't you need my car keys?"

Ryan was nowhere in sight. Slight sounds of crunching reached her and faded. Pounding on the loading dock door would get some attention If she needed help. Hopefully, the dishwasher wasn't so loud it would drown her knocking out. Kate sat down and started counting. "One monkey. Two monkey." How long did she wait and count?

Ryan stayed close to the building until he reached the edge of the illuminated corner and part of the parking lot. Shielding his eyes, his wolf vision adjusted. Shadows no longer hid things. Moonlight and starlight outlined the cars parked along the back section of the parking lot close to Sadie's. A feral cat raced across the parking lot, ducking and darting beneath cars, chasing its mousy prey. A lone person stood in the corner close to Sadie's rear entrance. Their head tipped back as if they watched the heavens for a sign. Their life outline emitted blue and gold sparks, possibly with each breath they took. Blue and gold life lights belonged to matchmakers' genetics. What matchmaker awaited him at Sadie's?

Ryan cautiously sprinkled part of the remaining ice melt in front of him. Several parking spaces and open lot separated him from the person at Sadie's rear entrance and his and Kate's parked cars. Two steps forward. Crunch. Crunch. Sleet hitting the ground mixed with the crushing of ice melt as he stepped forward bit by bit, pace by pace. The ice melt would run out before he got midway through the open parking lot. Shifting was out of the question. Would the person outside Sadie's hear his howl and come to help? Or would they bolt, fleeing, scared a wolf was close by?

Ty tossed his empty take-out cup in the dumpster. He thought his ears would never stop ringing. Karaoke night and howling seemed to partner up. Siobhan started watering down the beer an hour earlier. Holiday season, two full moons, and now the sleet storm. Icy roads and sidewalks by the time Sadie's usually closed. Could he convince Siobhan to close early? Mitchell's text that Ryan and Kate were on their way back to Sadie's alerted him to move the cars double parked in front of theirs. Ty pushed off the wall, took a look around the parking lot and back across the side of The Cove's building. Who was the person standing there?

NINE

"You need help?" Ty called out, moving closer to where the back parking lot light lit up the open area.

"Sure do." Ryan edged back under the circle of light behind him. "Ran out of ice melt. Not sure how slick it is between you and me."

Ty clicked on his mag flashlight, shined the beam over the patch between him and Ryan. "Wet patches. Black ice loves to lurk. Kate okay?"

"Yeah. She's waiting for me on the loading dock." Ryan moved two steps forward. "I'm going to get my car, pick her up, and take her to her car."

Ty nodded. "Stay put. I'm going to get the golf cart Siobhan keeps in the shed and come and get you. It's going to be a few."

"Got nowhere to run to. Have no notion of wrestling with black ice. I'm staying put." Ryan glanced behind him. He could work his way back until he was up against the building.

Ty called out as he moved back into the darkness near Sadie's back steps. "Suggest you get up against the building. Makes it easier to get closer to you with the cart and less chance to slip."

"Agreed." Ryan inched his way back to the building, leaned against the wall and slowly exhaled. Wolves were supposed to be nimble, sure-footed animals. He bet his wolf half wouldn't do so great on ice, much less black ice.

Ty pulled the shed door open. He didn't have to wait long for his eyes to adjust to the moonlight shining through the skylight dome. The white canopy and frame stood out in stark relief compared to the darker items stored further back in the shed. Getting the cart out, no problem. Getting it back in wouldn't be as easy. Damn cart didn't always stop smoothly when you hit the brake. He'd deal with that after he got Ryan.

Ty started the cart and put it into gear. He slowly inched out of the shed. Pings sounded as ice and rain hit the cart's metal top and front. Partway out of the shed, he turned on the cart's headlights. Great, low beams at best. Better than no light at all. Halfway across the parking lot, he sighted Ryan, hood up and tight to the wall.

"I'm going to turn around and get as close as possible. Get in the back and hang on." Ty called out, passing Ryan.

Ryan shoved his hands into his jacket pockets. The drip off the roof and the wind blowing caused the sleet to pelt him and soak his jacket. He hoped his gym bag was still in the trunk. Shivers and goosebumps, he didn't need. His nose itched. His eyes watered every time he sniffled. Catching a cold wasn't the issue. Sneezing as he clamored into the small box bed of the cart could throw his balance off. Landing on his ass on the ice wasn't an option cuz getting back up might not happen. Crawling across the parking lot on his hands and knees probably wouldn't work either.

"Ready?" Ty pulled up beside him.

"Yes." Ryan grabbed hold of the metal poles supporting the cart's roof. He swung one leg up, pushed off the wall with his other, and heaved himself through the small opening between the poles. "In."

The cart lurched forward as Ty put the cart into gear. "Hang on. We're headed for the back steps."

Ryan grabbed the back of the passenger seat and hung on. Slips and slides. Bumps and a few curse words later, Ty banged the front end of the cart up against Sadie's back steps. "You okay?"

Ryan slowly let go of the passenger seat. "I doubt you're that bad a driver normally."

Ty chortled. "Police academy 101 hazardous driving passed and then relearned when I attended Cauldron Falls police training."

Ryan snorted. "You mean shape shifter getaway training. You duck and get on the back roads as quick as you can."

Ty held his hand out. "Take it easy getting out. There's a slick spot close to the stairs."

Ryan gripped Ty's hand and put one foot out on the pavement. Then his other, slowly standing up. "Thanks. I appreciate the help. I can cut across the grass behind my and Kate's cars."

"Let me get some ice melt. Put it down between the cars. That way you got footing to get your door open and get in."

Ten minutes later, Ryan started his car. Ty gave him a thumb's up and rushed inside. They both agreed getting people to their cars and home safely meant closing the bar early.

Kate paced across the loading dock and back. Fourth time. Twenty-five steps and turn. Twenty-five steps back to the steps leading into the parking lot. Steps that were wet and dark. How slick and slippery, she didn't know. Texting Ryan could distract him as he made his way across the parking lot. How much longer did she wait? Mitchell had checked on her. He'd heard nothing from Ryan. The Cove was closing early. The storm and wind chill would make the roads icy and impassible.

Kate looked at her phone. No text. Another ten minutes had passed. Did she start down the stairs or go back inside? Spur of the moments crap. . .no planning. . .no discussion—Kate pressed her lips together. Mimicking her mother, Ryan's aunts, or any other relative that felt the need to tell her or Ryan how to live their life could go suck fifty extra sour lemons without any sweetener.

She stood up, descended a couple of steps looked out over the parking area. No sign of Ryan or sounds of a car approaching. Kate turned, ready to head inside and call Ryan to pick her up out front of The Cove.

"Need a ride?" Ryan asked, pulling up to the steps.

Kate turned around. "Praise Lupa, you're okay."

"Pretty much. Come on, get in. It's warmer with the window up." Ryan chafed his arm.

Kate dashed to the car. She pulled the door shut and turned toward Ryan. "Mitchell said to let you know they're closing early. Weather report is calling for two inches of ice and wind chill of below zero."

"I caught the forecast waiting for the car to warm up." Ryan closed the window. "Sadie's is closing too. Roads are dicey and getting worse. We've got a decision to make."

"Decision?" Kate held her hands out to the vent close to her, warming her hands.

"Better off traveling together. Who's place is closer?" Ryan put the car into gear.

"What about my car?" Kate fastened her seat belt. "Do we need to let Siobhan know?"

"Already discussed. We can leave one car here. Come get it when roads improve." Ryan pulled to the edge of the parking lot exit ramp. "Your place or mine? We're cohabiting for the next couple of days."

Kate let go a deep sigh. She glanced at Ryan. "Our second unofficial date."

Ryan snickered. "Yup. Hell of a way to start getting reacquainted."

"My place is out on Mallard Drive. Yours?" Kate pressed her fingers against her legs. Her psyche could stop chortling and smiling like a certain Cheshire cat from her fave children's book.

"Mage Ridge, a bit further out than yours." Ryan eased onto the street. "I've got some clothes with me. My gym bag is in the trunk."

Kate thrust one hand out toward Ryan. "Hello roomie. Hope you don't snore."

Ryan clasped her hand and let go. "If I do, it's not loud enough to wake me."

Kate snickered. "We're about twenty minutes from my place. Two more questions need negotiation."

"Oh?" Ryan glanced at her as he slowed for the yellow blinking traffic light blowing back and forth in the wind.

"Together or separate?" Kate sat up. "You got protection?"

Ryan wet his lips. Some people would call what was happening good luck, blessings and fortune smiling on them. Deity's sense of humor could be screwy at times. His answer would have to wait. Seeing out the windshield took priority.

"I'll answer that when we get to your place." He gripped the steering wheel tighter. "Snow wasn't supposed to fall until closer to dawn."

Snow mixed with sleet fell against the windshield.

"We're going to have to take the back way into the parking garage for my duplex." Kate's muffled curse echoed his apprehensions.

"We're coming up on Main. Where do I turn?" Ryan pumped the brake slowing the car even more. A couple of other cars passed them three intersections back.

"Turn right at Opera Alley. It'll take us between the courthouse and the entrance to the hospital parking lot." Kate shifted in her seat. "Second left as we pass the hospital parking lot is the entrance to my parking area."

"Got it. You watch street signs." Ryan turned on the high-beam headlights.

Five minutes felt like fifteen plus until they rolled partway through a deserted intersection. Ryan pumped the brakes, praying and hoping the weather didn't worsen.

Kate opened her window. Wind blasted into the car, rocking it back and forth. "Sorry. Needed to see the street sign and the business name."

"Is okay." Ryan slowly pressed the gas pedal. "We close to turning?"

"Yes, next intersection is our turn. It's where the street lamp is." Kate closed her window. "Street sign is on the lamp post. Not easy to see."

Thankful no other cars were approaching, Ryan rolled into the right turn, hoping Kate's place wasn't much further.

The speedometer read five miles per hour. Sides of the buildings loomed up, dark and eerie, like they could close in on them at any moment. Mortals believed supernaturals and magics didn't fear. Little did they know. Fear could take any form, conjuring up illusions that shook you to the core of your dualistic being. Ryan inhaled and exhaled slowly, keeping his gaze fixed on where the headlights illuminated the road. Staying in the moment kept fear at bay. Riding alongside it meant focusing on the task at hand. Too many dark moments murmured and muttered in the background. They and his wolf could snarl at each other all they wanted. He was in control, and getting through the alley was his top priority.

Kate leaned forward. "The first entrance is still lit. Go ahead and turn in there. We'll have to weave through the parking lot until we reach the second row of garages."

"Turning in is easy. Let's hope the lot is treated or we are going to be inching along." Ryan flipped on the flashers, turned the wheel and pressed on the gas. He crossed his fingers as the car lurched forward, tires spinning. Would they make it up over the ice and slush coating the parking lot apron?

TEN

"Hold on, we're going in." Ryan uncrossed his fingers, clutched the steering wheel tighter, and pressed on the gas.

Back and forth. Tires spun, sending ice and slush flying. He pressed on the gas a bit more—ready to try a different tactic than sitting with the back of the car hanging out in the street.

"Try again. Except steer to the left." Kate opened her window. "I can see a break where the other cars went earlier. If we follow their tracks, we might make it over the ice and slush build-up."

"Worth a try." Ryan glanced in the rearview mirror and side mirrors. No cars coming. "Here we go."

He backed up several feet, turned on the high beam lights and put the car into gear. Sounds of tires spinning came through Kate's open window.

Kate waved her hand up and down. "Back up a bit to your right. We're not quite in the tracks."

"Okay." Ryan backed up a bit more. Ice and slush flew into the air. The car rocked back and forth. The rear end fishtailed to the right.

Kate sighed. "If we don't make it this time, we'll have to park on the street and walk in."

"Sit back." Ryan checked the car was in gear and pressed the gas pedal like he was accelerating from stopping for a red light. The tires spun, and ice chunks flew up as the car rocked back twice. He revved the engine again, ready to take his foot off the gas pedal. Sounds of tires squealing, and the smell of hot rubber filled the air. The car shot forward, sending ice, snow and slush flying. Ryan pumped the brake, steering the car into an open area of the parking lot away from other cars.

Kate closed her window and laid her hand on Ryan's arm. "I-I. . .wow?"

Ryan nodded and grinned. "Yeah, wow. Right or left to your parking garage?"

"Left. Third one from the end. I'll have to get out and enter the code." Kate let go of Ryan's arm. They were safe. The car was fine. She wasn't questioning which one of her prayers got answered. She looked up, silently mouthed thank you and took several deep breaths. Maybe her heart and breathing would catch up to each other by the time she needed to enter her garage code.

She focused on her breathing and relaxed against the seat as her heartbeat returned to normal. Ryan slowly maneuvered the car in and out of open spaces between cars, moving toward her garage. She knew one thing. After they got inside, she wasn't venturing out until the weather broke.

"If you can pull close enough to let me out near the keypad, I can enter it while you position the car." Kate unfastened her seat belt.

"I'm glad the lights are still working. Be careful." Ryan pulled close to the garage.

Kate got out, watching where she walked. The patches of the pavement looked dry. She knew from experience to scuff the toe of her shoe sole across part of the possible dry spot. Scuff. Step. Scuff. Slide. Step to the side. Scuff another patch. Step. Ten more scuffs, followed by eleven steps, and she was at the keypad.

Kate entered the code and pressed open. The keypad blinked twice. Nothing happened. Kate entered the code again and pressed down hard on the open button. The keypad darkened as the garage door slid open.

"Go on inside. I'll pull the car in." Ryan backed the car up, waiting until Kate was inside close to the steps leading into the duplex.

Pulling into the garage, he noted how empty it looked. No yard tools or patio furniture. The walls were bare. It was like Kate hadn't settled in. De'Andre and Josef said she'd moved back to town eight months ago. Why hadn't she unpacked?

Ryan turned off the car and opened the door. "Your garage is bare. No yard tools. No patio furniture."

Kate took her keys out of her fanny pack. "Renting doesn't let you junk up the place."

Ryan got his gym bag out of the trunk along with a couple of grocery store plastic bags. "Junk up? Certainly, a few patio chairs and a few yard tools aren't junking it up."

Kate hurried up the steps. "Renting with an option to buy makes you think twice about how much stuff you really need."

Ryan nodded as he made his way up the steps. "Well, if you decide you want to buy, let me know. My cousin Sophia is a realtor. She'd got quite a few listings."

"Yeah, thanks." Kate pushed the button near the door to close the garage door. It clanged as it shut.

Ryan clasped Kate's arm. "Are you nervous?"

"Tired. Frustrated and nervous . . .maybe a bit." Kate pulled her keys out of the lock. "You're wet. Maybe tired too. I want to get your clothes in the dryer while the electricity is still on."

"I can wear my gym clothes. Let's go on inside. Hang my jacket on the back of a chair. We can hang up my jeans and shirt in the bathroom. Air dry overnight as best they can."

Kate stepped into her home. Her refuge, her sanctuary and. . .Ryan was right behind her. Her safety zone was breached. Not in a vicious way. In a way, she hadn't anticipated. She agreed to dates. Here was their second, like it or not. Good thing she'd gone to the grocery two days ago.

"Welcome to my humble abode." Kate hung her coat on the coat hook near the door. "The fireplace works. Plenty of wood. Solar power."

Ryan eased past her, nodding. He pulled off his jacket and hung it on the back of the chair close to the table. "Small and cozy."

"Yeah. Don't need much room." Kate folded her arms tight against her.

Ryan set his gym bag and the two grocery bags near the table. "Kate, you've got nothing to fear."

"The old Ryan I knew may not be the current Ryan. We're getting reacquainted."

"Then why did you ask me here if you're scared." Ryan sat in the chair he'd hung his jacket on.

"Scared isn't what I'm feeling. Unsure, yes. Weighing what I've learned so far. Not wanting to risk either of us getting hurt." Kate kicked her shoes off. "You've grown and changed. I'm intrigued. Is there more than chemistry happening?"

Ryan nodded. "I get it. I'm feeling the same way. This Kate is a strong independent woman. Someone who is willing to go after what she wants and protect herself at the same time."

"You sure about that?" Kate filled a tea kettle and put it on the stove to heat.

Ryan smiled. "Yeah. You challenged me. You didn't let me sweep you up in the moment and declare a full moon match. You kept your head about you."

Kate took two mugs out of the cabinet. "Right now, I need a hot drink. A snack and a question I asked you in the car answered."

Ryan stood, walked over to where his gym bag and the two plastic bags sat on the floor. He picked one bag up, walked back to the table and sat down. "A hot drink and a snack I can use too. As to one of your questions..." Ryan reached in the bag and took out a box. "Protection. Condoms. I carry two in my wallet and replace them well before the expiration date. I believe in protecting me and my partners. We're both responsible for that."

"Thank you for sharing." Kate dropped a tea bag in each cup. "My main concern is respecting boundaries. Neither of us needs to be pushed outside our comfort zones."

Ryan placed the box back in the bag. "Agreed. Warm cuddles would be nice. Shared warmth in case the electric goes out. A few hugs and a peck on the cheek good night is fine."

Kate snorted. "True shared warmth is better than a cold lonely bed. But—" She looked away.

"But you aren't sure that's all that's going to happen." Ryan held out his hand. "You know no one in my pack shakes on a deal and goes back on it. I'm offering to shake and establish agreed-upon boundaries for sleeping and tonight. Tomorrow we can renegotiate if you want."

Kate poured water into the mugs. She placed two cookies on a plate. She set the plate on the table. "Give me a moment, okay?"

"Sure." Ryan broke one of the cookies in two and popped a piece into his mouth.

Kate sat the mugs on the table. Did she agree? Her heart skipped a beat each time she thought about cuddling to Ryan. Knowing another person was present added to her feeling of well-being. Anyone else but Ryan wouldn't be here. *You trust him,* her psyche nudged. "If I agree, there's one thing. My bed is a queen. Not a whole lot of room. There is a small guest room with a daybed."

Ryan sipped tea, set the mug down, and wiped his hand on his jeans. "Queen is good. Room to cuddle and sprawl. I'll help with getting extra blankets on the bed. I even can cook." He held out his hand again.

Kate pulled a chair over close to Ryan. She sat down, cupped her hands around her mug. "Ryan, there's something I need to tell you."

Ryan scooted his chair closer. "I'm listening."

"There's another reason I left town." Kate sipped her tea. "Remember the one-night stand we had about six weeks before you left for New York and Europe?"

"Yeah. That is one of my fondest memories of our time together." Ryan laid his hand on the table near hers.

"Three weeks after you left, I found out I was pregnant. I couldn't tell my parents. They were set on me going to college and being the first in my family to get a degree." Kate dunked a cookie in her tea and ate it.

"What happened?" Ryan drank more of his tea.

"I miscarried a month after I moved. I was in the hospital a week recovering. The doctors said they weren't sure I could get pregnant again." Kate toyed with her mug, turning it back and forth. "It's okay if you want to sleep in the guest room."

Ryan stood and closed the space between him and Kate. He slipped his arms around Kate's shoulders and hugged her tightly.

"Kate, you're amazing. One, you went through a traumatic experience with few people you trusted around you. Two, I didn't leave you a way to contact me to let me know. If anyone is a fuck up, it's me. Can you forgive me?"

ELEVEN

"Can I forgive you?' Kate pushed her mug away. "Shouldn't I be asking can you forgive me?'

Ryan squatted down next to her. "Maybe we need to forgive each other? Our selves?"

Kate pressed her lips together. Had she done that? Forgiven everyone else but herself? Had she forgiven Ryan? She looked at Ryan. "I think I have. I might of. Some days I'm not sure."

Ryan stood. "I'll let you in on something. I thought about you a lot while I was gone. When I got back and found out you were gone, I wanted to kick myself. I knew I let a good thing go. A friend and lover who understood me."

Kate exhaled slowly. "I realized you were the best friend I never acknowledged. Maybe we needed to go apart to grow and appreciate what we had."

"Had?" Ryan asked, holding out his hand again.

"We possibly still have." Kate clasped Ryan's hand and squeezed it. She let go as she continued speaking. "I'm comfortable around you. I don't feel like I need to hide. Yet, there is much of me you don't know. The me that I grew into. The me I am now."

"Tonight, I'd like to hold you. I'd like you to hold me. Cuddle together in a warm bed, knowing that we're here for each other." Ryan picked up his mug, downed the rest of the tea in it, and set the mug in the sink. "I'm looking for acceptance and healing."

Kate put the cookie plate and her mug in the sink. "We both need that. Accepting each other where we are today. Who we are now. Building on the foundation we've already got."

62

The lights flickered as Ryan picked up his gym bag. "Hope you got flashlights handy. I'd race you up the stairs, except the lights would probably go out."

Kate chuckled. "Drawer behind you. There's matches in there too. I've got a few candles upstairs plus an extra flashlight. Quick wash up and in bed is next."

Ryan pulled open the drawer as the lights flickered again. Lupa, were the deities pushing them to the next level? Sleeping together? He clicked on the flashlight, adjusted its beam and clicked off. One or two books of matches?"

"Two. One for bathroom and one for bedroom if needed. We'll use the candles sparingly. Make sure they're out before we sleep." Kate held his two bags from the pharmacy.

The lights flickered again. Ryan shook his head. "I think we're getting a signal. Upstairs, go to bed and cuddle."

"Could be." Kate moved toward the stairs. "Hope flannel nightgowns don't stop you from hugging."

Ryan tittered and smiled. "Same could be said for red gym shorts and a paisley t-shirt."

"Well, you can't be missed with that outfit on. Nor would anyone want to rip off your gym stuff." Kate started up the steps.

"Gray shirt and shorts work better. Sweats same way. Now paisley underwear..." Ryan's voice trail off. He caught Kate's sputter and snicker as he followed her up the stairs.

Changing the mood might work for tonight. Morning might be different. It might not. For now, he was letting things be. He slowly exhaled and stepped up on the landing at the top of the steps. Quick clean up. Brush teeth and into bed.

Kate opened the closet close to the bathroom. She took out two towels and washcloths. She turned, waiting until Ryan stepped onto the landing. "Small guest is first door on the right. Next door is the bathroom. My room is the last door."

"Weren't these places originally supposed to be one bedroom and a den?" Ryan moved up beside her. "Housing for Cauldron Falls' proposed university?"

"Yes. When funding fell through, they offered them as duplex townhouses. Option to turn part of the living room into a downstairs bedroom never took off." Kate flicked the hall overhead light on. "Best get lay of the hall while we have light."

"Lead the way, ma'am." Ryan stepped into the hall. "At least before we get another signal from you know where."

Kate cleared her throat. "Not tempting any deity or fate. Two full moons, a blue one, and solstice plus Sadie Hawkins—I say we keep our thoughts on getting to bed and sleeping. Too much magic and love sparks bouncing around."

"Yeah, our luck, we got gobsmacked by both, twice over." Ryan clicked on the flashlight he carried. "Just to be sure."

Kate chuckled, pointing at the open door they passed. "Bathroom. If lights stay on, there's a night light in there."

"I'm keeping the flashlight handy regardless."

"Good idea." Kate stopped in front of the last open door at the back of the hall. "My room. Extra blankets are in the chest at the foot of my bed."

Ryan hesitated. "Unusual question. Who goes in first?"

Kate shrugged. "One of us has to. Door isn't wide enough for both of us to enter together."

"Uhm, how about you first since it's your space?" Ryan faced her.

"I already invited you in. Go ahead." Kate straddled the doorway, one foot in the hall, her other in her bedroom.

Ryan started into the room. He paused, turned around and moved tight to her. "A thank you kiss." He brushed his lips over hers. "And a good night kiss. Thank you for trusting me and sharing your space with me."

Kate grabbed Ryan's shoulder. "Kisses returned are good things. A thank you kiss for your thank you kiss." She pressed her lips to Ryan's. She traced his upper lip with the tip of her tongue and pulled back. "And the second of good night kisses. Possibly more to come."

Ryan puckered his lips this time. Kate slid her hand up Ryan's shoulder until her fingers touched his hair. Cupping his head with her hand, she leaned in, lips partially open. Would Ryan deepen the kiss this time?

Ryan waited until Kate's gaze met his. "Full hands don't let me hold you and kiss you like we both want."

Kate pulled back. "Sorry."

"Nothing to be sorry about. Let's get our hands empty and our arms full of each other." Ryan entered the bedroom and put his bags on the bed. He sat down and opened his arms wide. "I'm ready if you are."

Kate sat beside him, laying the towels and washcloths on the bed. "Cozy and ready."

Ryan slipped his arm around Kate's waist, hugged her tightly and leaned toward her. "Let's ignite those sparks."

Kate pressed her lips to his. She moved closer, pressing tighter to him. Ryan parted his lips, savoring the warmth and feel of Kate close and in his arms again. Kate's tongue met his. Tag and chase. Tasting, caressing and savoring each essence flowing every time their tongues entwined.

Kate laid her hands on Ryan's shoulders. Warm, strong muscles bunched and caressed her palms with each move either made. Sliding her hands along Ryan's shoulders until she reached his neck. Strands of his hair rubbed across the tops of her hands. Soft, silky to the touch, and . . . Kate pulled back, breaking off the kiss.

"Ryan, I need to slow down." Kate lowered her hands.

Ryan's breath warmed her face. "Okay. Something wrong?"

"Either the lights flickered again. Or those sparks turned into lightning bolts." Kate scooted back, creating space between them. "I think we need to get ready for bed before the lights go out."

One flicker. Two and—Darkness. Pitch-black darkness enveloped them.

"Either one of us got our wish granted or the storm's intensity picked up." Ryan's sigh cut through the dark silence quick and easily.

Kate patted the bed on her side and as far back as she could reach around her. "I don't care which one. I'm glad the bed is against an interior wall. Won't be so cold."

"True. What about your pipes?" Ryan brushed against her. "Trying to find the flashlight."

"Insulated. Running a trickle of water out of them overnight is probably a good idea." Kate touched a cold metallic item. "I found the flashlight."

She slid her hands down the cylinder until she found the on button. A bright beam of light illuminated the area around her and Ryan.

Ryan put up his hand between them, blocking part of the light. "Good. You said you got another one up here."

"Yes, in my nightstand drawer." Kate shined the light on the nightstand close to them. "Can you see where I'm shining the light?'

"Yeah. Do you want me to get the flashlight?" Ryan stood.

"Please. Top drawer, right-hand side." Kate held the flashlight higher, arcing the beam onto the nightstand.

"Got it." Ryan clicked on the flashlight. "I'll go down and turn on the kitchen faucet. Do we need anything from down there?"

"No. I'll get the blankets out. Do you want to wash up?" Kate rose.

"Yeah. There's save water shower with a friend." Ryan kissed her cheek and strode toward the door.

"We'd run out of warm water before either of us could get soaped and rinse. Better to both wash up at the same time. One in the tub. Other at the sink." Kate pulled two blankets out of the trunk at the foot of her bed.

"Gonna get naked and nothing more than soap and water happening. Some second getting reacquainted date, huh?" Ryan exited the bedroom, chuckling.

Kate smoothed one blanket on top of the other and turned down the top sheet and blankets back on both sides of the bed. She doubted anyone would believe they got naked in the same room and glanced at each other with flashlights while hastily washing and dressing for bed. Ryan was right. Their second getting reacquainted date was turning into a doozy.

Ryan checked the back door locks. Both were locked and bolted the same as the front door. He turned on both faucets and glanced out the kitchen window, noting the outside temperature.

Moonlit patches of ice decorated patches of the yard and tall oak and pine along the back fence. Snow swirled and blew across the yard with each chilled, windy blast. He opened the cabinet doors under the sink. If the temperature dropped much more below thirty degrees, the inside temperature might drop as well. Come morning, they might be curled tight to each other with the blankets wrapped around them.

TWELVE

Ryan turned over, opened his eyes, and quickly closed them. Sunlight streamed through the open curtains, bouncing off the dresser mirror and brightly spotlighting him and Kate. He opened his eyes again, squinting this time.

Kate lay on her side, facing away from him. If he moved much, he'd jostle her. They'd settled in to sleep somewhere around midnight. He grinned as images from last night's rush to get ready for bed came back.

Candlelight, water trickling out of the tub faucet and Kate at the sink in all her delightful nudity. Him buck assed naked in the tub. Kate corrected him twice. He was nude like her. Chilled water and soap didn't contribute to hot once-overs. Hell, if he'd had a hard-on, cold water hadn't helped it. If he'd had a hard-on, he didn't notice. He was too busy moving around to keep from chilling more.

Ryan smiled at bits and pieces of his and Kate's conversation he remembered. In bed, clothed, teasing to warm cold hands and feet on each other. Agreements on talking more about Aunt Stella and Aunt Agatha's Christmas dinner. Kate's sleepy acknowledgment that attending as friends made sense.

He flexed his shoulders and arms. Cool air rushed under the blankets.

"If you're that hot, get out from under the covers." Kate turned on her side, facing him. "In case you're wondering, I'm awake."

68

"I didn't think you were talking in your sleep." Ryan stuffed his pillow under his head. "I'm debating getting up or running to the bathroom and darting back to bed."

"One of us is going to have to go first." Kate uncovered one arm. "Burr."

Ryan tossed the covers off, stood and took off at a trot toward the bedroom door. "I'll be quick. Hope the toilet isn't freezing."

Kate pressed her lips tightly together. Mirth lurked, waiting to burst forth. She knew firsthand about blatantly waking up sitting on a cool toilet seat. Last night it was all she could do to keep her teeth from chattering as she squatted to use the toilet. She hoped that Ryan didn't encounter as cold a toilet seat.

Last night felt and seemed unreal. She and Ryan had shucked their clothes in front of each other. Used the bathroom together. Even managed a few kisses and a couple of hugs in between trying to keep warm and finish getting ready for bed. She didn't think he'd notice the large t-shirt she pulled on. He had. His old double xl shirt he'd given her from one of the places he visited in Europe. Soft, worn and roomy made sleeping all that much more comfortable.

Nude hugs without any fondles. If anyone had told her this happened with Ryan, she'd never believed it unless she were there. She was and it happened. Even after they'd gotten into bed, nothing more than a few more hugs, some talk and a kiss on the cheek. Ryan hadn't made a pass at her. She hadn't at him. Not that the thought hadn't crossed her mind. They'd struck an agreement and stuck to it.

Kate rolled on her back and stretched. The air didn't feel as cold as it first had. Since the sunlight often warmed the room and the mirror reflected the light back into the room, the temperature stayed warm during the day. She sat up and scooted to the edge of the bed. When Ryan came back, she'd take her turn using the bathroom.

Ryan hung his washcloth and towel up. Cleaning up went quicker this time. The heat had come on as he entered the bathroom. Warmth as he cleaned up felt much better than last night's cold air. Maybe later, he and Kate could grab warm showers. For now, lazying in a warm bed with Kate held a lot of appeal. A few kisses and cuddles added in would be nice. He'd put the box of condoms on the nightstand. Being prepared mattered. No surprise pregnancies needed. Kids were cool. He wanted them after he pair bonded or full moon matched. Possibly legally hitched too.

Kate met him at the bedroom door. "Heat came on."

"Good. I'll check the solar panel gauge when we go down for breakfast." Kate patted his ass and entered the bathroom.

Ryan opened his mouth, closed it, and shook his head. He'd gotten a good morning ass pat. Not exactly an item his usual good mornings had. Then sipping coffee and going over the day's menus with Mitchell and Ben while sampling the daily breakfast pastries didn't offer opportunities for good morning ass pats from a woman he wanted patting his ass.

Kate smirked as she entered the bathroom. Patting Ryan's ass had caught him off guard. Good! She liked morning affection. Nothing overly gooey unless there was time like today to cuddle, kiss and—who was she fooling. She liked gooey morning affection too. Long slow kisses that led to morning loving. Hot steamy hugs that promised of more to come or turned into moments of tenderness filled with sweet whispered words of affection. That was how she'd like her mornings to be. None of her relationships had gone there. The guys she'd ditched with over-inflated egos left her vowing to not jump into another relationship until she was sure. Why was she taking a risk with Ryan?

Ryan she knew. Or did she? She wanted him to learn about who she'd become. Didn't he deserve the same respect and option? Wasn't that why he was here? She could have driven herself home.

Or gone to a motel. She and Ryan could have done that too. She was taking the risk because she was doing the detective work on Ryan as well. Well, before she and Ryan had shown any interest in each other, Josef and De'Andre had mentioned him and others she knew before she'd moved to Witchita Springs. Curiosity piqued her more than once about the man who'd snagged her heart and interest.

You gonna mess up the opportunity? Her conscience could show up at the dangest times.

Nah, that's not it. I'm voicing what you're thinking. You want to go for it. You know you do. What are you waiting for? A sign. I think you got one.

Kate finished washing up and brushing her teeth. She hung her towel and wash cloth next to Ryan's. She looked in the mirror, pointed at her reflection and murmured, "I'm gonna take a chance. Listening to my heart and risk being vulnerable." If she didn't know better, she'd swear her reflection winked at her.

Ryan was stretched out in the bed, leafing through one of the magazines she kept on the bottom shelf. "Anything interesting?"

Ryan laughed. "Article on social media postings. How to handle nosey people. How posting provocative things can get you hits on your post or put in social media jail. Not my thing."

Kate got back in bed on her side. "Bottom shelf is ones that need tossing. I don't get social media either. Advertising is important. Blasting speculations and false info doesn't help."

Ryan put the magazine back on the shelf. "Yeah. My marketing manager steers clear of that stuff. Local advertising is plenty for me. National coverage isn't needed."

Kate turned toward Ryan. "Change of topic."

"Okay." Ryan turned on his side, facing her.

Kate folded her pillow under her head. "Do you want me?"

"Why are you asking?" Ryan didn't look away. It was like he stared at her, watching and waiting.

Kate tried to swallow. No luck. Her throat sucked all the wetness out of her mouth. How did she explain her. . .fear? Curiosity? Need to know? Or was that her fifteen-year-old self asking because insecurity howled in the depths of her memories?

She inhaled slowly, pressed her lips together, and sighed. "A part of me needs reassurance. More, I want to know it's okay to say I want you. There's a need to know. Mutual desire is a great catalyst igniting passion, desire and chemistry."

Ryan moved closer, laying his hand on her waist. "Yes, I want you. Have since I asked you to see the matchmaker with me. I don't screw and disappear. I'm a lover. I care about the person after the chemistry dissipates. It takes two for mutual satisfaction."

"Then why haven't you. . ." Kate stopped talking. If she'd voiced where her thoughts were going, she'd sounded like she was out to score and nothing more. Deities, why had telling someone she desired them become so hard?

Ryan cupped her face. "I haven't because I need to know you want me too. I can get off by myself if that is all I want. I need and want more. Your pleasure is part of my pleasure. I need to hear your yes I want to as well. I respect you."

Kate draped her arm loosely along Ryan's waist. "I desire you too. Screw 'em and leave 'em is not my style. That is taking. Not giving. Pleasure, like you said, is a two-way thing. Get, give and get again. Knowing you can bring another person pleasure is so much more intoxicating than just a fast orgasm and jump back in your clothes or turn over and sleep."

Ryan slid his hand down her neck, across her shoulder, until he came to her breast. He moved his thumb back and forth over her nipple. "Enough talking. Let me show you what you do to me."

Ryan lowered his hand to Kate's. "Here's what you do to me."

He guided Kate's hand down over his hip until he reached his groin. He nudged and rubbed against her hand.

"I get you hard." Kate cupped his balls and cock. "I turn you on."

"You sure do." Ryan pulled his t-shirt over his head and tossed it on the foot of the bed. "We've got too many clothes on."

"I can remedy that." Kate started pulling one arm through a sleeve.

"I'd rather undress you myself." Ryan nipped the bare flesh between Kate's shoulder and neck. "Pull the shirt part way up. I love to explore."

Kate bunched the shirt up to her waist. She lay back.

"Arms over your head." Ryan tossed the covers off her. "While I'm exploring you can help me undress some too."

"How am I supposed to undress you if my arms are over my head?"

Ryan winked, lowered his head close to her ear and whispered. "When I say it's okay. Slow and easy builds the need."

She gulped. "I don't like D and S play."

"Honey, no D and S happening. Focusing on your pleasure first enhances mine. Prolonging adds to the build-up." Ryan suckled her ear lobe between his lips, worrying it with his teeth.

THIRTEEN

Ryan slid down the bed until he was level with Kate's exposed stomach and mons. He puckered his lips around the tip of his tongue, leaned forward and traced the outer edge of Kate's navel. He looked up. Kate watched him. Part of her shirt pulled tight over her taut nipples. He was getting a reaction. Good.

He rose on his knees, placed his hands on either side of Kate, and blew on her wet skin. Small jerks and soft moans resulted. "Luscious. Beautiful."

Ryan straddled Kate. "Wonder what's next?"

"Maybe. You might do the opposite if I guess anything."

Ryan grinned. "Could be. You'll have to wait and see."

He slowly made his way down Kate until he could see her vulva. "Spread your legs."

Kate shook her head. "What if I don't want to?"

"And miss out on my kissing your clit? Laving my way over and around your tastiness? You've given up oral sex?" Ryan stuck his tongue out, flicking it back and forth several times.

Kate jerked and moaned. Oral sex with Ryan was one thing she remembered in vivid detail. Her swollen clit pulsating every time he licked. Up. Down. Back and forth. His lips capturing her clit and not letting go as she arched against him. Pressing tighter to him. Her hands cradling his head. And...

Ryan inserted two fingers into her, slowly thrusting in and out. "Oh, your g spot is right where I remember it being."

"Oh." Kate lowered her arms. "You gonna keep teasing?"

74

Ryan worked his fingertip in slow circles around her g spot. "Who's teasing? You're deliciously wet and ready for me to sample your sweetness."

He licked both fingers, then his lips. "Nectar fit for more tasting."

Ryan lay between Kate's legs. His arms around her legs, cradling her hips and ass. He licked one thumb pad, then his other. He slowly parted her vulva, exposing her moist hard clit. He blew across it, settling lower between Kate's legs. He glanced up. Kate had worked her shirt off. She cupped her breasts, raising them as she ducked her head. Her lips puckered. She captured one nipple. Then her other. Ryan shifted, trying to find a spot where the crotch of his shorts and his balls plus his cock weren't fighting over space. He swore he couldn't get any harder.

He ducked his head and licked. Quick rapid tongue flicks over and on Kate's engorged clit. Lick. Suck. Two fast licks. Suck and two finger strokes across her g spot.

"Ah! I'm—I'm..." Kate's hands clutched his head, jerking toward him. Wetness coated his tongue and fingers. Salty yet sweet. Kate tasted as wonderful as he remembered.

Ryan wiped his face with the sheet. "You're beautiful when you orgasm. Sheer pleasure watching you come."

Kate let go of the sheet she had bunched in her hands. A deep breath. A slow exhale. Her fantasies were nothing compared to what just happened. Ryan was one damn fine lover.

"I think part of me is still up there." Kate pointed at the ceiling. "I been missing out. Should have grabbed you the night of the dance and had my way with you."

Ryan moved up beside her. "Friends with benefits is good stuff. I prefer lovers with benefits."

Kate patted Ryan's cheek. "When chemistry is this hot, you need to ignite the catalyst as often as possible."

"There's a slow fuse that needs help." Ryan took her hand, slid it down along his leg.

"No fair. You got naked without my help." Kate feathered her fingers through Ryan's pubic hair.

"You got your shirt off without my direct help. So I did the same with my shorts." Ryan moved his hips back and forth, rubbing his hard cock against her hand. "Now, about that slow fuse."

Kate cupped her hand around his balls. Warmth oozed over his balls and pooled around his cock, drenching and soaking deep into him. Desire's catalytic spark hit his flame of need and desire.

"I like your response to my touching you," Kate whispered hotly against his ear. How much more before he exploded? Could he last long enough to get a condom on? Not at the fuse's current burn rate.

"I do too." Ryan shifted slightly on his side. His cock followed, laying itself more fully against Kate's palm. Lupa, if she decided to taste him—"Ah-hh."

Kate stroked upward and across his cock head, rubbing his leaked wetness down and over him. She coated him from tip to base, tight to his balls. She rose over him, closing her hand around him. "Let's see if you taste as good as I remember."

Ryan couldn't have closed his eyes if he wanted to. Something he dreamt about, fantasized about and fervently wished for was happening.

Kate puckered her lips, opened them like she was going to french kiss Ryan, and leaned down. One lap. One kiss. Another lap lower until her lips closed around Ryan. Suckling and licking commenced. Rapid tongue flicks across his glans. Over around and back until . . .

"Much more, and I am going to come." Ryan cupped her head, holding her steady. "I'd much rather share mutual pleasure."

"Condom?"

"Right here." Ryan held up an open condom packet. "Help me get it on. You decide the position."

Kate grasped Ryan in one hand, the condom in her other. Slow and easy or quick and fast might not get the results they wanted. Too quick, and the condom tore. Too slow, and Ryan might lose his hard-on. She glanced at Ryan, blew him a kiss, and worked the condom down and over him.

"Yeah, we didn't tear it." She straddled Ryan, scooting back until his glans and her mons touched each other. "Me on top is our best option."

Ryan nodded, placing his hands on her waist. "Allows me to stroke your clit at the same time."

Kate shivered. Stroking her clit as she rode him would intensify her orgasm. If Ryan thought a prolonged session would happen, he better think again. Well, again, after post-orgasmic bliss got done with them.

Rising on her knees, she guided Ryan into her. Fullness. Fullness she missed. None of her ex-lovers filled her like Ryan did. She rose slowly, tightening as she did. She leaned forward, placed her hands—palms down—on the bed and began rocking back and forth.

"I'd forgotten how good you feel inside me."

"Let's make some new memories. Ones that I don't intend to stop making or let you forget." Ryan wet two of his fingertips. He stroked down between Kate's mons until he met wetness. Two fast rubs across Kate's clit followed by slow circles over and around her clit, coating her with her wetness.

"Oh, I'm close." Kate started rocking back and forth quicker. "Much more, and it's going to be *intense*."

Ryan clasped her hips, meeting her thrust for thrust. They met and.
. .

Reds, yellows and bursts of green outlined Ryan. Her eyes closed as array after array of colors, like fireworks exploding in the night sky, filled her vision.

Kate tightened around him, holding him snuggly inside her. She pulsed with each orgasmic contraction. Much more and...

"Oh, Lupa! I'm coming." Ryan arched his neck, sucking air in through his open mouth. Pulse after pulse of orgasm pumped through him, reaching deep into his heart. Igniting a blast of heartfelt joy and sureness.

Kate slowly opened one eye. She lay atop Ryan. His breath warmed her face. She tried to raise her head. "I don't think I can move."

"Me either." Ryan wrapped his arms around her. "We'll try in a few moments. Just soak in the bliss and energy."

A few more moments passed. Kate raised up on her elbows, yawning. "I'm ready to sleep."

"Me too." Ryan yawned. "Gotta separate so we can, and I can get the condom off."

Kate rolled off Ryan and onto her side.

Ryan patted her cheek and sat up. "I'll be back in a few."

Kate moved to the edge of the bed, sat up and pulled her sleep shirt on. She stood, tossed back the covers and crawled in. Ryan got in beside her. His t-shirt and shorts back on. Kate smiled as she closed her eyes. Maybe this reacquainting thing was worth pursuing.

Buzz! Ring! Buzz! Ryan rolled over and reached for his phone. Who was calling and texting him? He blinked and sat up as he glanced at his phone. Two texts and three missed calls. His phone buzzed and vibrated. He set the phone back on the nightstand. Blinking more, he stared at the clock on the nightstand until he could clearly see it. Noon! Last time he had checked the time, it was seven-thirty, just after sunrise.

"Kate, you awake?" Ryan lay back on the bed, yawning and stretching.

"Some. What's up?"

"I missed a lot of calls, or service was out." Ryan sat up again. "Checking my messages and voice mail."

Kate stretched. "Okay, I'm going to shower and dress."

"I will join you in a few." Ryan scrolled through his messages. Malia and Debbie asking him to call. Aunt Stella was on a rampage about dinner not being finalized. He smiled as he listened to his voicemails. Aunt Stella cussed him out about not getting back to her with what the menu was for sure. Debbie's message was a repeat of her text. Malia's voicemail said Aunt Stella wanted him to come over right away. He laid his phone on the nightstand, shucked his clothes and stretched. He'd get back to them after a shower and breakfast.

Twenty minutes later, he and Kate sat at the table sipping coffee and eating breakfast. His phone had buzzed and rang three more times. He glanced at the caller id each time it rang. Aunt Stella could stop sitting on her burr and demanding his attention. He'd be there as soon as he was ready. Not before.

FOURTEEN

Ryan put the car into park. Sitting in Aunt Stella's drive less than six hours after he and Kate made—oh no, he wasn't using that word yet. They agreed to keep their hearts out of things until they had more time to talk. Like either of their hearts was going to listen. On the drive, stuck in traffic and even two blocks away, temptation dangled memories from this afternoon's intimacy.

Kate blissed out. Her arms around his neck. Her kiss tempting him to go for round two, possibly three. . .Then his blasted phone had to buzz, ring and chime. One right behind the other. Malia's text. Debbie's voicemails and the missed phone call from Aunt Stella. What had put Aunt Stella into terror mode? Not afraid. Wielding her position. Barking out orders to quote Malia. Debbie called, whispering in her voicemail that Aunt Stella was demanding to talk with Ryan now. Something about dinner plans still not finalized. Lupa, had Aunt Stella's mind gotten so bad that she couldn't remember she approved the main menu choice along with the backup menu?

Ryan got out of the car. He grabbed his portfolio out of the middle console and slammed the car door shut. Let that announce his arrival. Kate offered to come with him. He said no. Aunt Stella would start with the nosy questions and not stop until she got what she considered a satisfying answer.

Malia met him at the top of the back porch steps. "Ryan, I'm glad you're here."

"What burr stung Aunt Stella now?" Ryan wiped his feet and entered the back porch sunroom enclosure.

80

"Aunt Agatha and Derek arrived this morning. She challenged Aunt Stella to top ten matches, including hers and Derek's." Malia leaned close, lowering her voice as she continued. "I've been calling all the guests on the list who hadn't RSVPed yet or indicated they were coming with a date or match."

Ryan rolled his eyes. "And Debbie?"

"Calling The Cove looking for you. Chef and Pierre asking what they knew about the meal menu." Malia perched on the arm of one of the chairs on the porch. "We tried telling Aunt Stella that Aunt Agatha was plucking nerve."

"Sibling rivalry at its best." Ryan dropped into a chair opposite Malia. "These two have been trying to one-up each other since they were kids. This time we need to head them off. Put a lid on this."

Malia nodded. "Debbie and I agree. But how?"

"How many did you get a hold of from the guest list?" Ryan took the pen out of his portfolio.

"Ten out of the twenty listed. Why?"

Ryan tapped his pen against the portfolio pad. "Have you talked with Aunt Agatha's assistant Felicia?"

"Briefly, a couple days ago."

"Did she say how many were coming?"

"Ten. Maybe twelve. That wasn't including dates or matches." Malia sat in the chair opposite him.

"Derek and Agatha plan on getting married on New Year's Eve. How about we surprise them with an early pair bonding ceremony?" Ryan scribbled two sentences on the pad.

"How are we surprising them?"

"Surprise is the matchmaker presiding over the ceremony is Chef's second cousin, Tracey. Her husband Ralph is Sylvan Valley and Cauldron Falls' justice of the peace." Ryan showed his pad to Malia.

"Oh, that's devious." Malia nodded. "Aunt Stella gets the honor of hosting the ceremony at her house. Aunt Agatha and Derek get a flashy event in front of family members and guests. It might work."

Ryan laughed. "Aunt Stella loves surprises. Aunt Agatha loves being the center of the party. Together they get both, and the family pulled one over on them."

Why was Malia frowning?

"What if this backfires? They start arguing."

"Have you ever known Aunt Stella or Aunt Agatha to blow up at a family event?" Ryan could name one time.

"One family wedding rehearsal. They didn't speak to each other for months."

"Correct. We let Aunt Agatha and Aunt Stella think there's a contest going on to see who will end up with the most pair bondings or matches made at the dinner." Ryan pressed his lips together. Hopefully, he and Kate weren't going to need to fake that.

"Malia, is Ryan here yet?" Aunt Stella called out.

Malia slowly stood. Ryan snapped his portfolio shut. He laid a hand on Malia's shoulder. "We best go in. We'll talk about this more later. Do you think you and Debbie could meet Felicia and I at The Cove around four this afternoon?"

"Possibly. I'll see if Aunt Stella's neighbor can sit with her for a couple of hours. I'll need to bring back Mrs. Beckwith's dinner and some other goodies. Payment for services rendered."

"Mitchell will make sure there's enough to feed Mrs. Beckwith's family and dinner for you, Debbie and Aunt Stella." Ryan paused at the steps leading into the house. "Has long has Aunt Stella been in this mood?"

"Since Aunt Agatha called to let her know she and Derek arrived." Malia entered the house. "To say Aunt Stella's been on a terror is an understatement if you know what I mean."

Ryan chuckled. "Oh, I do. She is miffed, frustrated and eager to figure out a way to upstage Aunt Agatha."

"For sure." Malia closed the patio door behind him. "Do you want coffee or tea?"

"Neither. I had a late breakfast." Ryan toed off his shoes. "At least we can keep Aunt Stella focused on the menu when she sees our shoes are off."

Malia nodded, grinning as she pointed to the shoe rack near the patio door. "No need to wipe up wet floors. In-floor heating is working. Comfortable and safe."

Ryan entered the dining room, glancing around the room. The long table took up the front third of the room. Setting the infamous folding table next to the main table once the table leaf was in place would fill two-thirds of the dining room. The ceremony would have to take place in the living room. He jotted a note on the paper on top of the portfolio and stuffed the paper in his jeans pocket.

"Hi, Aunt Stella." Ryan kissed his aunt's cheek. "Sorry, it took me longer to get here. The roads are still icy."

"The storm. People should have sense enough to stay home when that happens." Aunt Stella pointed to the couch across the room from her. "Sit down. Malia will get us some coffee."

"No thanks." Ryan sat on the couch. "I brought the menu and the backup menu with me. I thought you made up your mind."

"Don't question me, Ryan Butler. If I want to make changes, I will." Aunt Stella glared at him.

"Look, I know Aunt Agatha and Derek are back." Ryan pulled both menus out of the portfolio. "How about you and Aunt Agatha have both families here for Christmas dinner?"

"There's barely enough room for everyone at either house." Aunt Stella pointed at Malia. "Malia, please get me the RSVP list."

Malia winked at Ryan as she walked past. Ryan handed his aunt the agreed-upon menu. "The main course is Turkey and dressing, baked salmon with dill sauce, and maple honey glazed ham. The sides are mashed potatoes, gravy, mixed roasted vegetables and an assortment of salads."

"Yes. Were you able to order everything?" Aunt Stella handed him back the list.

"I was. Meat arrives tomorrow morning. Siobhan kindly offered me the use of her roasting oven to do the turkey and the vegetables. Chef and Pierre are already making the breads and desserts." Ryan put the menu back in the portfolio.

"We don't need the backup menu." Malia sat in the chair between the couch and Aunt Stella's wingback chair. "What about a progressive dinner? We meet here for the first and main course. Then go over to Aunt Agatha's for dessert and after-dinner drinks. Maybe play some board games."

Ryan nodded. "I like that idea, Malia. Nobody is left out. Aunt Agatha can't outdo you, Aunt Stella. You get the first round with the appetizers and main course. You get to make the first impression on all those attending."

Aunt Stella glanced at him and Malia. "Outdoing Agatha is getting harder every year. There's still who's got the most matches."

"Aunt Stella, what if you and Aunt Agatha did your tallies at her house? You announce your total. If yours is greater, you win and show Aunt Agatha up in her own house." Ryan stuffed his hand in his jeans pocket and crossed his fingers.

Aunt Stella looked down, then back up, smiling. "One up and out doing Agatha in her own house. She might not talk to me for a while. Still, I love the idea."

"Okay. I need to meet Mitchell at The Cove and check on things. How about Debbie and Malia meet me there around four to plan this out more?" Ryan stood.

"I'll check with Mrs. Beckwith about sitting with Aunt Stella." Malia stood next to Ryan. "Dinner from The Cove sound good, Aunt Stella?"

Aunt Stella grasped Ryan's hand and tugged. Ryan leaned down. "What do you need?"

"One of Mitchell's fancy burgers with mushrooms in a salad. Soup too. Enough for Mrs. Beckwith, Malia, Debbie and me." Aunt Stella let go of Ryan's hand. "And Ben's ice cream."

"Aunt Stella, only soup for the rest?" Ryan leaned down and kissed his aunt's cheek.

"No, burger and mushroom salad for all of us. Maybe some crackers and cheese too." Aunt Stella sat up straighter. "Go on, Ryan. Hurry up. Can't keep Mitchell waiting."

"Right. That much sooner you get to feast." Ryan hugged Aunt Stella. "I get it."

Malia walked out onto the sun porch with him. "I haven't seen her perk up this much since Felicia's call about sighting Ethan Hunter at the market."

"Her old beau?" Ryan stepped out on the steps.

"Yes. Aunt Stella kept denying her interest in Mr. Hunter." Malia held her finger to her lip. She glanced back at the open back door. "Felicia said Aunt Agatha muttered something about her biggest and best match would be getting Aunt Stella and Mr. Hunter back together."

"Never a dull moment with Aunt Agatha and Aunt Stella." Ryan stepped onto the sidewalk. "I'll check with you in a few about meeting and if I got the dinner order right."

Malia waved as he pulled out of the driveway. Two of Cauldron Falls' oldest, supposedly retired, matchmakers trying to outdo each other. He hoped that he, Malia, Debbie and Felicia could pull off surprising the two aunts with a tie in outdoing each other this time.

Ryan put his bluetooth headset in and dialed Felicia's number. She answered on the second ring.

"Hey Ryan. What's up?" Felicia's voice sounded muffled.

"Did I catch you at a bad time?"

"No." Felicia's voice got clearer. "I'm loading packages into my car. Been out running errands."

"Okay. Can you meet Malia, Debbie and me at The Cove around four?" Ryan pulled up to a stop sign.

"Should be able to. What's going on?" The sound of Felicia's trunk closing sounded in the background.

"It's about time us cousins pulled one over on Aunt Stella and Aunt Agatha. One where they end in a tie trying to outdo each other." Ryan grinned at Felicia's laughter.

"It's going to take some secretive planning. Can't wait to hear what you got in mind." Felicia started her car. "See you at The Cove at four."

Ryan eased into the turn on Main Street. Could the four cousins outwit their aunts? Pull one over and let the aunts think it was their idea?

FIFTEEN

Kate glanced at the clock. Three hours since Ryan left. His last text said to meet him at The Cove at four. She had ten minutes to get ready and leave. Ben and Mitchell had brought her car back. They reported the roads were passable for the most part. Ice storms were notorious for leaving lasting mementos like black ice. Wearing her hikers made sense. Would Ryan be coming back with her? Stay another night? They still had much to talk about.

She put her lunch dishes in the sink, glanced out the kitchen window, and nodded. The sunlight was waning, indicating she'd need to be sure to have her heavier coat with her. Two days until Christmas. Two days till she and Ryan had to have their reacquaintedness finished enough to pull off their renewed coupledom. Deities on high, magic was no help with matters of the heart. Aura reading magic helped some. There were still patches of uncertainty and the fakers whose aura said one thing and their actions another.

She trotted up the stairs, unsure how to calm her heart, much less the butterflies flittering in her stomach. The meeting at The Cove might illuminate an idea or two from what Ryan's first text said.

Eleven minutes later, Kate wrapped her neck scarf around her neck, zipped up her ski jacket and checked her hikers double-knotted laces. She picked up the small bulging pouch sitting next to her fanny pack. Amethyst, jade, and bloodstone plus three other crystals filled the white and silver pouch. In her left jeans pocket, obsidian and sunstone crystals rested. The white and silver pouch would guide her as she sat at the table listening to what Ryan and

87

the others had to say. She might not need extra protection or to enhance her third eye aura reading abilities. Going into the unknown, she felt armed and ready to use her magic as needed.

"They're here. I seated them at the table close to the front." Mitchell carried a tray laden with croissant sandwiches and a pitcher of Ben's special tea blend, Christmas Holiday.

Ryan pushed the swinging kitchen door open. "Thanks Mitchell. Is Kate here?"

"Ben saw her pulling into the parking lot about five minutes ago." Mitchell stopped a few steps into the dining area. "You might want to go meet her. She called Ben, asking questions. He didn't say what they were. Just that she sounded apprehensive."

"Understandable. She doesn't know more than the cousins are meeting." Ryan stepped back into the kitchen. He made his way toward the load dock door. "Ben, let Mitchell know Kate and I'll be in in a few, please."

"You got it, boss man." Ben saluted him and took off through the kitchen door.

Kate opened her car door. Ben's vague responses weren't helping. No matter how many times she repeated his one main answer, she wasn't calming down. Ben repeated twice he didn't know what the meeting was about. She'd have to ask Ryan. Would Ryan think she didn't trust him if she called him and asked what was going on?

"Need help?" Ryan stood in front of her. "Everyone else is inside."

"I can get out on my own." Kate exited the car. "It's what is waiting inside I am not sure about."

"Unknown, got it. Cousins meeting, got it." Ryan squeezed her hand. "We're plotting how to pull something off on Aunt Agatha and Aunt Stella."

Kate locked the car. "Please tell me this is not the you need to go to the old magics' home talk."

Ryan shook his head. "Nope. We all know better than that. I still wince when I remember the verbal scolding we all got the first and only time that came up."

"Me, too." Kate shoved her hand into her jeans pocket. She clenched the obsidian and sunstone and let go. "You know those two are going to figure something is going on with all of us here."

Ryan stopped at the loading dock steps and faced her. "That is why we're telling Aunt Agatha we're working on helping her get one over on Aunt Stella and vice versa."

Kate pointed at Ryan, pressed her lips together, and blinked. Luna and the One help them all if the aunts found out before the prank went off. Kate clapped her hand over her mouth hoping she kept her laughing down.

"Yeah, we got some serious planning to do on this." Ryan bounded up the loading dock steps. "Aunt Stella's old beau Ethan Hunter is back. He's asked about Aunt Stella several times, according to Felicia."

"I'm intrigued." Kate clasped Ryan's hand. "Let's go see what we can come up with."

"Okay, we're all here." Ryan sat next to Kate. He placed a croissant sandwich on a plate and passed it to Debbie. He kept on until everyone had one.

"Help yourself to tea." He filled a glass for himself and one for Kate. He waited until all had their glass of tea. He raised his as he spoke. "Here's to pulling one over on Aunt Agatha and Aunt Stella. And getting them and their beaus pair bonded."

Felicia rapped on the table as Ryan set his glass down. "Aunt Agatha's guest list is ten pairs. They all decided to pair up. A few said they're not letting Aunt Agatha tinker with their matchmaking."

Debbie raised her glass. "I'm for choice. We've all felt the full moon match urge and the Sadie Hawkins sparks. How many let the matchmaker make the choice anymore?"

"Not many, cousin." Malia touched her glass to Debbie's. "I know quite a few on Aunt Stella's guest list have found dates. Malia and I told her we were coming as each other's date."

"I bet that got her to sputter and not saying much." Kate sipped her tea.

"Actually, we've got a couple of guy friends showing up. It took Aunt Stella several moments to process the response." Malia took a bite of her croissant sandwich, chewed and swallowed. "She said as long as no one got hurt, sexual choice and match choices should be left up to those involved."

Ryan tapped on the table. "All right. Let's get back to how we're going to do this. We're in agreement on the progressive dinner idea?"

"Debbie and I are." Malia finished her croissant and sipped her tea.

"Sure are." Debbie wiped her mouth. "Let Mitchell know the croissants are awesome. I hope they make a hit on the breakfast menu."

"Already have. These were part of the last batch Ben made right before lunch." Ryan popped the last of his croissant into his mouth, chewing as he nudged Kate.

"Huh?" Kate glared at him.

"What do you think of the progressive dinner idea?" Ryan wiped his mouth. "Main course at Aunt Stella's. Dessert and games at Aunt Agatha's."

"How does that pull one over on them?" Kate finished her tea and croissant.

"We get them pair bonded at Aunt Stella's as we mingle after finishing dinner. Announce the reception is at Aunt Agatha's," Felicia offered.

"Maybe get Aunt Agatha and Derek pair bonded at Aunt Stella's and Aunt Stella and Blake at Aunt Agatha's." Kate glanced at Ryan. "Or both of them pair bonded on the car ride between houses?"

"Hmm," Ryan began. "You might have something there. We've invited Tracey and Ralph O'Shay. One could ride with Aunt Stella and Blake. And one with Aunt Agatha and Derek."

"Ralph is a justice of the peace. Not a third coven witch or mage." Kate glanced at Ryan. "You've got a good idea. It's witnesses and the right person officiating."

"Felicia, did Tracey and Ralph rsvp to your invite?" Ryan opened his portfolio and started writing. "Progressive dinner is doable. We know how Aunt Stella and Aunt Agatha hate cleaning up."

"Wait," Malia called out. "We could do dinner here. Have the full moonlit arch set up and tell them there could be a surprise pair bonding or two happening. Christmas is the last full moon night until after New Year's."

Ryan nodded. "Everyone gets a goodie bag of leftovers to take home. Group clean-up would work. Everyone pitches in with serving and setting up before Aunt Stella and Aunt Agatha get here."

Kate snapped her fingers. "Oh and here is the surprise. Tracey and Ralph have the pair bonding paperwork ready for Aunt Agatha and Derek, plus a set for Aunt Stella and Ethan to fill out and sign."

"Are we good then with meeting here early, setting up, and getting Aunt Agatha and Aunt Stella here separately?" Ryan made two last notes. He passed sheets of paper around the table. "Here is what we've come up with. Make a copy for yourself and reach out to the guest lists by midday tomorrow."

"I'll get Aunt Agatha and Derek here." Felicia folded her note copy in half and stuck it in her purse. "Aunt Agatha invited Blake. He RSVPed this afternoon. He'll ride with them."

"Malia and I will make sure Aunt Stella gets here." Debbie handed Malia her note copy.

"I'll get Tracey and Ralph here." Kate leaned toward Ryan. "Hard part is convincing each aunt that they are setting the other up."

"Very true." Ryan kissed Kate's cheek. "That's Malia, Debbie and Felicia's job."

"Ryan, did you kiss Kate?" Malia winked at him. "Are you two back together?"

"Not officially." Ryan nudged Kate. "We're friends contemplating benefits."

"*Ryan!*" Kate glared at him and glanced at the others. "We're friends. The benefit part is we're getting reacquainted."

"Oooh, do I sense an announcement?" Felicia grinned.

"Don't know what you mean." Ryan stood. "Kate and I are old friends getting caught up with each other. Where that goes is between us, okay?"

Debbie, Malia, and Felicia nodded. Debbie spoke as she and Malia rose. "Most of the guests are taking the magical fourth amendment too. No telling what ain't theirs to tell."

Kate shoved her hand in her coat pocket, fingered the crystal pouch and said, "Ryan and I are rediscovering each other. Where that goes, we aren't sure. Friends is a good description."

Another fifteen minutes passed, confirming Felicia, Debbie and Malia's next steps. Each would text Ryan the updates on the guests and how their conversations with Aunt Stella and Aunt Agatha went.

"Walk you to your car?" Ryan handed Kate her coat.

"Thanks." Kate slipped her jacket on. "I've got a couple of questions."

"Go ahead." Ryan held the loading dock door open.

"Are you coming back tonight? Is friends with benefits enough?" Kate started down the loading dock steps.

"Depends on if you want me back tonight." Ryan paused. He waited until they were at the bottom of the steps. "Benefits are negotiable. We can talk about that tonight if you like."

Ryan pulled Kate into his arms. He brushed his lips over Kate's. "Think on it. I'll call you with my answer later."

SIXTEEN

Kate rolled over, stretched and sat up. Christmas morning. Ryan's soft snore sounded behind her. She smiled, stretching again. Up late two nights in a row, talking, laughing, and cuddling. Two nights she never imagined would happen. Ryan and her holding hands, agreeing to be present in the here and now as much as possible. Reuniting meant reacquainting with who they were now.

She stood and quietly exited the bedroom. Last night's discussion had turned vocal when Ryan asked if she'd were his ring. Not an engagement ring. A promise ring. A symbol of their intent to give being a couple another try. Ryan told her not to worry about what others read into the ring. If someone asked, she could say they were working on things. She didn't want either of them subject to gossip and family pressures like they were as kids and young adults.

Kate closed the shower curtain, turned on the shower, and began to soap up. One thing Ryan said she totally agreed with. Neither of them was dependent on family. Gossip mongers were going to chatter no matter what anyone did or said. She glanced at her right hand. The solitaire ruby surrounded by emerald clusters adorned her ring finger. She'd promised as Ryan slipped the ring on her finger; she would do her best to focus on what they wanted plus where they needed to be.

"Got room in there for me?"

Kate jumped, tossing the soap at Ryan as he entered the shower.

"Who else did you think it would be?" Ryan caught the soap, stuck his hand under the shower spray, and began working up a lather.

94

"Caught up in my thoughts." Kate ducked under the shower, rinsed and tried to move past Ryan.

"Wash my back, please." Ryan held out the soap. "You worried about if the condom broke last night?"

"Some." Kate rubbed the soap over Ryan's shoulders and down across his ass. "If it did, it did. We cross the bridge to parenthood as necessary."

"True." Ryan turned around. "What else you thinking about?"

"Our agreement." She held up her hand. "This and what it symbolizes."

Ryan brushed his lips over hers. He laid his soapy hands on her shoulders.

"It symbolizes what we want it to. Nothing more. Nothing less."

"Part of me still cringes over the gossip crap I went through moving back." Kate rinsed again and exited the shower.

"I wish your grandmother hadn't tried to keep your family together at her expense." Ryan shut the shower off and pulled the curtain back. "I'm sorry you had to go through that alone."

"Thanks. I wasn't alone, per se. Certain money-hungry relatives and their need to be part of the elite tiers of Cauldron Falls society spent money none of them really had." Kate hung her towel on the rack. She handed Ryan his towel.

"You aren't alone now. I'm here for you as you need me to be." Ryan finished drying and hung his towel up next to hers.

"Thanks, I appreciate it. You're a gem I cherish, and am glad you're part of my team." Kate exited the bathroom.

"Glad to be part of it." Ryan followed Kate into the bedroom. "I've been thinking about what you said last night about moving away to find ourselves."

Kate tossed underwear, jeans and a pink-mauve striped turtle neck sweater on the bed. "Oh?"

"Yeah, I needed to find out what I wanted and who I was. Going overseas opened my eyes and tastebuds to new cuisine, new outlooks and taking a chance on trying something new and different." Ryan pulled on his briefs and t-shirt. "Learning to cook more than toast, eggs and oatmeal ignited a keen understanding of taking care of me."

"Eating your own cooking can be boring if you don't have cookbooks." Kate smiled and ducked as Ryan tossed a pillow at her.

"Smart mouth." Ryan laughed. "I enjoy creating new recipes. Taking existing recipes and enhancing them. Unique blends and outcomes."

"Is there more cooking that needs to be done?" Kate finished dressing.

Ryan tucked his dress shirt into his jeans. "No. Pierre and Chef have keys to get in and start the warming trays. They're bringing over the desserts and breads from Sadie's. Siobhan delivered the ham last night to Mitchell before we closed."

"All we've got to do is get Aunt Stella and Aunt Agatha to The Cove, right?" Kate tied her hikers and fastened her fanny pack around her waist.

"Tracey and Ralph arrived last night. Stayed at Aunt Agatha's after a brief visit with Aunt Stella. Neither knows they visited the other." Ryan threaded his belt through his jeans' belt loops.

"I'm helping Felicia get Aunt Agatha and Derek here. Our story is that Aunt Stella is hinting at proposing to Ethan Hunter at dinner and making a pair bond match." Kate shook her head. "I need coffee and food before I can do this with a straight face."

Ryan patted her shoulder. "We both do. De'Andre texted me that Josef is bringing Emily to dinner."

"Who's De'Andre bringing?" Kate entered the hallway.

"She's coming with Zack." Ryan started down the stairs.

"The pack's alpha?" Kate followed Ryan.

"Yes. All either of them said was it was a mutual decision." Ryan faced Kate. "We can eat at The Cove. I'll fill you in on what we told Aunt Stella on the way."

"We gotta let Aunt Stella and Aunt Agatha think they got some of these couples together." Kate zipped up her jacket.

"They did. We all paired up to come to dinner." Ryan laughed. "Maybe they pulled one over on us."

"I don't care at this point. Dinner with family and friends is a great Christmas present." Kate handed Ryan his jacket. "Knowing my benefit buddy is my date makes the event super fantastic."

"Same here." Ryan kissed Kate's cheek and opened the front door. Twenty minutes later, they entered The Cove.

"You told Aunt Stella you convinced Ethan to come to dinner?" Kate sipped her coffee. "But we don't know where Ethan is."

"Caleb from the matchmakers' council does." Ryan pushed his empty plate to the middle of the table. "Ben's eggs, cheese and ham croissants hit the spot."

"Glad he left some for us." Kate set her mug down. "Did you get a hold of Ethan?"

"Yes." Ryan picked up his mug, grinned and swallowed the last of his coffee. "Ethan is sitting in my office talking with Chef and Pierre. He helped them decorate the wedding cakes."

"*He what*?" Kate winced at the loudness of her voice.

"No need to yell." Ryan stacked their plates. "Ethan figured the best way to get one over on Aunt Stella is to propose and have the matchmaker and justice of the peace ready right beside him."

"You know we're never going to hear the end of this." Kate wiped her mouth and stood.

"Probably not." Ryan picked up their plates and entered the kitchen. "Let me introduce you to Ethan. Then we need to finish decorating, get our honored guests, and get celebrating."

Kate followed Ryan into the kitchen. Laughter and chatter flowed out of the office.

There was no mistaking Pierre's voice. "You must have thought twice about moving back to Cauldron Falls."

Kate and Ryan peered around the door. Pierre sat opposite a medium-set man with gray hair and a mustache. His glasses were on top of his head. He smiled as he and Pierre talked.

"Thought about more than twice, Pierre. You know when it's time to come home."

"Ethan, you're a world-class chef. Your cakes and desserts are renowned worldwide."

"Fame and fortune come and go. I've started and sold so many restaurants and pastry shops that I lost count. Moved around trying to find that elusive place I could call home." Ethan pulled his glasses down, adjusting them on his face. "After my fifth country, twentieth city, and rental places getting smaller or more expensive, I said enough. Time to come back where it all started."

Pierre nodded, turning as Ryan and Kate entered the office. "You did a great job on both cakes."

"Simple decorations, colors and font are all you need to make an impression." Ethan stood. "Ryan, when is Stella arriving?"

"Soon. Malia texted she and Debbie are picking Aunt Stella up in forty minutes." Ryan nudged Kate forward. "Ethan, I'd like you to meet Kate."

"Pleasure to meet you." Ethan smiled at Kate. "Stella's told me a lot about you."

Kate glanced at Ryan. "Hope none of it sullen my reputation."

Ethan chuckled. "Nothing other than bits and pieces about her nieces and nephews over the years."

"Well, I can relax." Kate glanced at Ryan again. "I think."

"Handshake? I promise to not tell stories about what I've heard or ask questions at dinner." Ethan moved around the desk, holding his hand out. "If you want to ask me what I know at another point, you're welcome to. I will tell you this, Stella is very proud of all her nieces and nephews."

Kate clasped Ethan's hand and shook. "I might take you up on asking what you know at another point."

Ethan nodded, smiling. "Happy to oblige."

Ryan glanced at his watch. "We got fifteen minutes to finish decorating and setting up the buffet and tables."

"Chef and I took care of part of that. He had to run over to his mom's for Christmas morning breakfast. He'll be back in time for dinner." Pierre rose. "The Moonlight Arch and bouquets are in the dining room."

"Good." Ryan looked at his phone. "Felicia texted she's on her way with Aunt Agatha and Derek."

"I talked with Agatha this morning before I left the hotel. She and Derek think they're going to pull one over on Stella." Ethan fished in his pocket, pulled out a small box and opened it. "I think I am going to pull one over on both of them."

"Beautiful ring." Pierre squeezed by Kate and Ryan. "Chef should be here along with De'Andre and Zack. Let's get finished up."

Ryan exited the kitchen first. Chef, De'Andre and Zack stood talking with Ralph and Tracey near the decorated arch.

"Ryan, can I talk with you a moment?" Ralph approached Ryan.

"Sure, what's up?" Ryan moved away from the others. Ralph followed him.

"It's about the marriage certificate forms and pair bonding forms." Ralph took them out of his portfolio. "Some are filled in already."

"What?" Ryan reached for the forms Ralph held.

"Hi. We're here," Debbie called out, entering with Aunt Stella and Malia.

"We're here too." Felicia followed by Aunt Agatha and Derek entered behind Debbie, Malia and Aunt Stella.

Ralph stuffed the forms back in his portfolio. "We'll discuss these later."

Ryan turned to greet his guests. Leave it to his aunts and Derek to arrive early. So much for extra in-town holiday traffic.

SEVENTEEN

"Welcome, Aunt Agatha." Ryan embraced his aunt. "Great, you and Derek could be here."

Ryan offered Derek his hand. "Derek, how was your trip?"

"Short and icy." Derek shook Ryan's hand. "The drive from Sylvan Springs was fine. Once I got into Cauldron Falls, the roads got icy. Told Agatha it's time I move in with her."

"*Derek*," Agatha chided. "TMI. Everyone doesn't need to know."

Ryan laughed. "Aunt Agatha, we've known for years you and Derek spend weekends together several times a year."

"Beside Agatha, we're engaged." Derek gave Agatha a side hug.

"Agatha, you were always the showoff." Aunt Stella moved to the front of the receiving group. "Blabbering about you and Derek shacking up."

"Stella, I am not." Agatha faced her sister, hands on her hips.

"Aunt Agatha and Aunt Stella, please, no bickering. It's Christmas."

"Besides Stella, it's time you tried some of that shacking up."

Stella turned around, her mouth open.

"Yes, I'm here." Ethan walked over to Stella, kissed her cheek and dropped onto one knee. "Gotta do this proper."

Ethan clasped Stella's hand. "Stella, let's shack up. Be pair bonded. You know, get engaged and hitched."

"Ethan Hunter, you're asking me. . ." Stella couldn't finish speaking. Her mouth moved, but she didn't speak.

"Yes, I am proposing." Ethan held the box up. "Got your fave ring with rubies and moonstones."

"Ethan, are you sure?"

101

"As sure as having the justice of the peace and his witch wife here to solemnize everything." Ethan took the ring out of the box. "Say yes, Stella. I love you and want to spend the rest of our lives together."

"Agatha, we can't let Stella and Ethan outdo us." Derek clasped Agatha's hand. "Come on, we're getting hitched too. Tracey and Ralph can tie it up nice and neat. No need to worry about New Year's. We can be honeymooning instead in Hawaii. Warm honeymoon sure beats a cold icy wedding."

"Wait one moment," Stella began. "If we both get pair bonded and hitched, we're tied."

"Guess so." Agatha grinned and shrugged. She made a sweeping wave, pointing to the group behind her, Derek, Stella and Ethan. "We pulled one over on them too."

Stella turned around, looking at the group of cousins and friends, and back to Agatha. She laughed, nodded and said, "We sure did, sister. They all showed up with someone. They aren't spending the holiday alone."

Ryan glanced at Kate, Debbie, Malia and Felicia. "Guess the saying is true, you can't outsmart a matchmaker."

Ralph leaned closer to Ryan. "This is what I wanted to talk about. One license has Derek and Agatha's names filled in. Another Stella's and Ethan's."

"Are those legally registered?"

"Good thing nothing is legal until the couple signs and Tracey and I sign and notarize the license. Form can be filled out with names ahead of time."

Stella and Ethan stood beside Agatha and Derek as each couple exchanged vows. Tracey blessed the matches and unions as per the matchmakers' council decree that a thirteenth coven witch must bless and affirm the matches. Ralph solemnized the pair bonding marriages per the state, Sylvan Valley and Cauldron Falls laws.

Ryan faced Kate. "Aunt Stella and Aunt Agatha got what they want. Possible matches happening. We're pulling one over on them with getting them pair bonded and hitched. And they got quite a few Christmas reunions happening."

Kate slipped her arm around Ryan's waist, hugging him tightly. "Yes, and our reunion is one of them."

EPILOGUE

Ten Months Later

Ryan stood near the earth-tone-covered arch decorated with fall festival lights and a full moon. Sadie Hawkins effect in full swing. Sparks of magic filled the air, igniting bursts of color in firework arrays close to everyone in attendance. Several full moon matches were waiting their turn to pledge their future together. Thirty days weren't what he and Kate were pledging.

Cheers and applause erupted as Nick Morgan took the stage to the right of the floral-covered arch. Nick picked up his guitar, strummed two chords, and nodded. His accompanying band played the opening melody of Nick's latest hit, "Listen to Your Heart."

The ballad hit home for Ryan. Listening to his heart, hearing what Kate's heart said mattered. They risked hearing each other out. Had some humdinger arguments. In the end, creating the safe space to speak their truths led them here. Ready to make a lifetime commitment.

Proposing hadn't been easy either. Kate had turned him down flat twice. She asked him, and he said no the first time. It took them by surprise when they both said yes. A weekend away, not even Aunt Stella and Aunt Agatha knew about, from family and friends provided them the quiet place they needed to admit they'd never fallen out of love with each other. Their time apart had benefited them in growth and getting to know what they each wanted and needed. Then there were the two pink lines.

He didn't know who's mouth hung open longer. His or Kate's. Three months into the pregnancy revealed another surprise, twins. Neither he nor Kate knew of twins in either of their families until Aunt Agatha's genealogy search yielded a family genetic revelation. Prior multiple births were commonplace among shape shifter packs. The introduction of gene pools and species changed the birth counts.

Ralph, Sylvan Valley and Cauldron Falls' Justice of the Peace, walked up to the floral arch and stood slightly outside the center of the arch. "Thank you, Nick, for that wonderful song. Listening to your heart is an important part of pair bondings, full moon matches and marriage."

"Ready?" Ralph asked, opening up his portfolio.

"I'm ready." Nick stood beside Ryan. "Ryan, you ready?"

"Thanks for being my best man." Ryan shook Nick's hand. "I'm ready."

"Josef and I are glad to help." Nick let go of Ryan's hand. "Josef grabbed his part right off."

Ryan smiled, nodding. "Yeah, let's see how he does."

The crowd parted as the opening strains of the wedding march sounded. Agnes stepped into the opening, carrying a bouquet of white and mauve chrysanthemums. Her dress matched the flowers' mauve tone almost perfectly. Behind her came De'Andre wearing a periwinkle blue dress and carrying a mixed bouquet of varying blue-hued flowers.

"All, please join hands and form a semi-circle around the open aisle." Ralph moved under the arch with Ryan and Nick to his left.

A chord sounded, and a melody Nick wrote especially for Ryan and Kate began. Josef entered the semi-circle. Two steps in, he stopped and turned, holding out his arm and hand.

Kate stepped into the semi-circle pushing a stroller holding Estelle and Patrick, her and Ryan's twins. She moved up to Josef, accepted his arm and began her walk toward Ryan. Her crown of pink and blue flowers matched each of the twins swaddling blankets and outfits. Ryan hadn't seen her dress until she entered the semi-circle. Each piece of the dress came from wedding dresses her mother, grandmother and Aunt Agatha had worn for their weddings. The newest piece was the mauve and blue lace sash. Her addition to the dress.

Josef pushed the stroller to the right and stood close to the front of the semi-circle. Ryan met her as she stepped in front of Ralph. Ryan clasped her hand and winked at her.

"Kate and Ryan, do you have something to declare?" Ralph pointed to each of them.

Ryan and Kate faced each other. Ryan spoke first. "I, Ryan Butler, declare my love for you and our children. I commit to this pair bonding, full moon match and give myself in marriage to you."

"I, Kate Ferndale, openly declare my love and commitment to you and our children. I freely enter this pair bonding and full moon match and give myself in marriage to you." Kate raised their joined hands and kissed the back of Ryan's hand. Ryan kissed the back of her hand.

Ralph tied a silver and pale yellow ribbon around Kate and Ryan's wrists.

"May Luna and the One bless this union. May your love and commitment grow stronger and deeper. By the powers bestowed to me by Sylvan Valley and Cauldron Falls and the state, I pronounce you pair bonded, moon matched and married. Blessed Be!!"

Ryan slipped his arm around Kate's waist, pulling her to him. Her gaze met his. "Kate Ferndale, I had one wish for Christmas to meet up with the woman of my dreams. Thank you for making my wish come true."

Kate brushed her lips over his and pulled back. "Ryan Butler, you're welcome. Thank you for making my Christmas wish come true."

"I did?" Ryan cupped her cheek. "How so?"

Kate brushed her lips over Ryan's. "Yes. My Christmas wish was for a reunion with the man I've loved and cherished for a long time. You."

Both of them had gotten their heart's wishes, a full moon Sadie Hawkins Christmas Reunion filled with love and magic.

THE END

Don't miss out!

Visit the website below and you can sign up to receive emails whenever Solara Gordon publishes a new book. There's no charge and no obligation.

https://books2read.com/r/B-A-RAUJ-WTLKC

BOOKS 2 READ

Connecting independent readers to independent writers.

Did you love *A Christmas Reunion*? Then you should read *Believe In Love*[1] by Solara Gordon!

[2]

An invitation to a family wedding, nothing to worry about, right? Wrong! Solo attendance isn't a good idea

when the invitation reads guest plus date in bold letters.

Nick Morgan isn't about to give his Mom and Gram the opportunity to attempt to matchmake him with every

available supernatural female in Cauldron Falls. It's enough he's the only grandson without any supernatural

abilities. Sandra Cunningham is the one mortal who might agree to fake an engagement with him long enough

to attend the wedding.

---

1. https://books2read.com/u/m2QWer

2. https://books2read.com/u/m2QWer

Sandra agrees to Nick's plan when Nick commits to reciprocating for her family reunion.

Maybe her mother will stop her matchmaking attempts when Nick shows up with her. Catching the grandson of one

of Cauldron Falls' oldest supernatural families does have nice overtones.

When the fake proposal, ring and all, gets anonymously videoed and hits social media,

are Nick and Sandra ready to take things to the next level and believe in love?

Read more at https://solaragordon.com/.

Also by Solara Gordon

Cascade Bay
Love Reborn
Reunited By Choice
Love's Triple Play

Cauldron Falls
Believe In Love
A Christmas Reunion

Peyton Corners
Falling for You
Caught by Love's Slow Burn

Standalone
A Heart's Desire
To Love You Again
To Love You Again

Watch for more at https://solaragordon.com/.

About the Author

Solara loves and lives with her partner of 21 years in the Metro DC area. What started out as a bi-coastal romance soon settled on one coast.

A vivid imagination keeps her busy creating her next fascinating romance. She enjoys creating unique characters and watching their journeys unfold. "Love freely given multiplies and will return endlessly" is a key aspect of her stories. Add in alternative lifestyles and her love for the paranormal, and the uncommon becomes the norm in many of her stories.

Her day job in the financial services industry pays the bills while she pens her erotic tales.

Read more at https://solaragordon.com/.